AF256349

Ghost Stories, Witches, and More

© José Salazar Duarte2024

Kindle Direct Publishing

Paperback Edition 2024

J.J. Salazar

Ghost Stories, Witches, and More

Index

Prologue

What makes us human? What defines us as individuals and as collectives? What connects us to the past, the present, and the future? These are some of the questions that this book seeks to answer through the ghost stories and traditions of a Spanish-speaking country.

This book is not just a horror book, although it contains tales that will send shivers down your spine. It is a work that reflects the love, humor, drama, adventure, culture, and history of a people and their spirituality. It is a piece that unveils the soul of a Spanish-speaking country through its ghosts.

Ghosts are more than mere apparitions or supernatural manifestations. They are also expressions of memory, identity, creativity, faith, and the resilience of a people who have learned to coexist with the inexplicable. Ghosts are part of the lives of the individuals who inhabit this book, sharing their experiences, dreams, disappointments, passions, and sacrifices with the spirits of their land.

This book invites you to explore a world where the natural and the paranormal merge, where reality and fiction blur, where the ordinary and the extraordinary complement each other. Here, you can journey into a universe where the magical and the real intertwine, where the historical and the legendary meet, and where the human and the divine reconcile.

This publication opens the doors to Latin American culture in a way that will surprise, move, make you laugh, make you cry, and make you reflect. Do you dare to enter?

When the Little Bird Sings

Maracay, Aragua state 1943,

"Death is something we should not fear because, while we are, death is not, and when death is, we are not."

- Antonio Machado

In the darkness of that chamber, voices laden with concern echoed. "Poor child, so small and what a loss he has suffered," one of those present whispered. A tragedy loomed over the family like a fog that hindered clear thinking, rendering the moment of facing the child with the truth impossible.

"At some point, they will have to reveal it to him," another added thoughtfully, as if words could heal sorrow. The conversation flowed in a hushed murmur, a delicate dance between words, as if walking on a minefield of raw emotions and fears.

In the adjoining room, a child immersed in his own world of fantasy skillfully manipulated toy soldiers. That room was his refuge, where the clamor of reality had not yet disturbed his tranquil imagination. However, the mother, like a gentle breeze blowing through the curtains, intruded into that improvised sanctuary.

- Miguel, beloved son, – she murmured with a tone full of affection and concern. The child momentarily set aside his warlike thoughts and turned to his mother. What are you doing here? - she inquired tenderly, trying to comprehend the world he was creating.

- I'm playing, Mom, – the child replied innocently, as if each of his words carried a small particle of magic. I am a general preparing my troops for the great battle. Like Marlborough, who went off to war. But I will return, Mom. With my victorious troops and shining medals. I will marry a princess, and our love will be crowned in the majesty of France.

The child's words hung in the air, like butterflies dancing in the garden of his dreams. His eyes gleamed with the certainty of his own destiny. We will dance in Paris, you and I, – he continued enthusiastically. And my dad will dance with you while I spin with the princess, who will then be a queen. People will love us, Mom, because I will be a just and good King.

Then he continued, – And it will be just like that time when they celebrated my birthday at grandma's house, and I felt like I was going to burst from the amount of cakes I shared with my cousins. Do you remember that occasion? It was such a beautiful moment, wasn't it?

The mother's response came as a warm sigh, wrapped in nostalgia and love. – Yes, my dear, it was a wonderful day, – she whispered with a tender voice. Her eyes seemed to weave memories as she spoke. - And it was wonderful, in large part, because of you. Because you are an exceptional child, full of kindness and tenderness. Good children, like you, always receive special rewards from God.

The mother observed the child with a mixture of sadness and admiration. At that moment, she understood that the child's fantasies were his way of escaping the pain that life had thrown upon them. A pain that, sooner or later, they would have to face and assimilate. Meanwhile, in that corner of the room, the little general continued building his kingdom of dreams, a sanctuary where reality had no power to penetrate.

The gathering continued outside the room, while the child's aunt, with moist eyes, prepared the clothes that would accompany her loved one to his final resting place. "We'll put him in this dress," she whispered with a tremor in her voice, "it was his favorite. And here, these family photos, so he never feels alone."

The door remained ajar, allowing the entry and exit of neighbors with their condolences—some out of sympathy, others out of curiosity, and some offering help, ready to alleviate any need. In this bustling of souls, the sun faded on the horizon, and the time came to head to the funeral home to honor the departed. But before proceeding, an urgent matter arose: communicating the news to the child.

The grandfather raised the question that hung in the air laden with pain. - Who will take on the task of telling Miguel? - he asked with a broken voice. Then, an echo of a defeated and confused voice arose. - It's me who must do it, I volunteer, - was heard, a voice that echoed like a shared lament.

A gentle tap on the door of the child's room, followed by a voice requesting permission to enter. - Miguel, little Miguel, may I come in? - the voice asked tenderly. From his world of imaginary battles, the child responded, - Come in, but be careful with the toy soldiers, they are lined up for battle. The visitor entered cautiously, lifted the child, and sat him down besides, like a confidant.

- Son, – the man began with a faltering voice, – there's something I need to share with you. Something sad, for me and for the whole family.

The child's innocent and curious eyes locked onto his father's. – Dad, why do you have tears in your eyes? What's happening? – he asked with sincere confusion.

With a trembling voice, the father began to explain, trying to find the right words.

- You see, your mom has been sick. She has been suffering a lot. That's why God called her to take her to heaven, where she won't feel pain anymore.

We won't see her again, son – Tears rolled down the father's cheeks as he held the child tightly.

- Dad, that's not true, – the child interrupted, like a burst of hope amidst the sorrow. – My mom was here not long ago. She told me not to be sad, that she will watch over us and come for me when the little bird sings. – The child's response, infused with faith and belief in a magical world, left the man bewildered, in a meeting between the real and the imaginary.

Years passed; Miguelito grew up, formed his own family, and carved his own story. Life continued its course, with joys and sorrows. Time wiped away the tears and replaced mourning with the longing for a future. At 86 years old, Miguelito found himself facing his own end, sick and fragile in a hospital.

While his youngest daughter, named after his mother, was at her father's house, preparing some things, a noise captured her attention. Intrigued, she opened a cupboard, and from it emerged a beautiful blue bird that perched on the window sill. Its song echoed like a familiar echo, and in an instant, the bird took flight, leaving behind a melody of hope.

A shiver ran down the young woman's spine, connecting the pieces of a story that enveloped her since childhood. The phone rang, and the news came: - Rosaura, dad is gone, but his departure was serene, as if he were smiling. As she let go of the phone, a sad yet meaningful smile crossed her face, while her eyes rested on the window. "Because she will come for you when the little bird sings," she murmured, letting the magic of words and memories fill her heart once again.

Shame

El Baúl, Cojedes state, 1930,

"Before embarking on a journey of revenge, dig two graves."

- Confucius

In the tranquil corner of the Venezuelan plains, in the year 1929, in the town of El Baúl[1], a tumultuous event unfolded and shook the peaceful lives of its residents. Amidst the commotion and confusion, two figures stood out in the scene.

- Isn't that Don Benancio? - Marta whispered, her voice filled with concern. What is he doing with that knife? His shirt seems to be soaked in blood.

- Damn, Marta! exclaimed her companion, visibly disturbed. He's chasing his wife, the teacher. My God! I believe the blood on his shirt is from her. He stabbed her.

However, Marta couldn't simply walk away. Her instinct for compassion urged her to intervene:

- But she is in danger; we must help her.

- Damn it, let's get out of here. That's some down-to-earth couple trouble, and that guy is really stubborn.

---

[1] Town of Venezuela

The central figure in this drama was Mrs. Gloria, a woman of about thirty, with blonde hair and blue eyes, not very tall but well-proportioned—quite beautiful, indeed. Her roots extended to the Canary Islands, brought by her grandparents in search of a better life. They had arrived in the country at the beginning of the 20th century with the aim of seeking a better life, but they had chosen the wrong town, and amidst numerous civil wars and tropical diseases, they had become stuck in the high plains of the Cojedes state.

In her youth, Mrs. Gloria moved to the city of San Carlos to complete her teaching studies. At that time, it was not common for a woman to pursue education, but Gloria was more independent than the average women of her era. She returned to El Baúl to take care of her elderly parents and there she met Don Benancio, a prosperous town merchant, a rough man not given to displays of affection or romantic postures, also the owner of some lands which he scheduled according to his criteria. I mean by this that most of the land was unproductive because there were no regulations back then, as there are now, to compel landowners to maintain their lands for the common good. He, descended from hardy people who had been there since before independence and were the result of the union of the Spanish white, the Indian, and the black. People of mixed race, as Simon Bolívar[2]

––––––––––––––––––––

[2] Liberator of America

described Venezuelans on one occasion. With this description as a prelude, it might have been expected that Benancio would not be to Gloria's liking. However, in the 1920s, in a town like El Baúl, where the Main Street of the town was, as I would tell you, the entirety of the town, there weren't many options to choose from. Nevertheless, something that no one can deny is that Benancio was a man of his word and conducted himself properly within the limits of that time. He didn't take what wasn't his, didn't fail to pay his debts, and wasn't afraid of the devil himself.

In summary, allow me to tell you that between them, romance did not blossom, but rather it was a kind of business agreement. He provided the means, and in return, Gloria would assume the role of a devoted wife, ready to comply with whatever her husband determined. After a brief engagement period, they took the step towards marriage. However, his aspirations to keep her at home, following the trend of the time, clashed with Gloria's strong determination. She prioritized her teaching vocation over marital authority.

Gloria's days were divided between home and school. Her figure was loved and respected by the town's inhabitants. She stood out for her dedication, responsibility, and sincere concern for her students, whom she treated as if they were her own children. Although she maintained the firmness characteristic of teachers of that time, she avoided resorting to common coercive methods of those period.

The atmosphere at home was prosperous until one of those days when destiny seems to plot everything to turn adverse. Benancio was engrossed in a card game, and the air was thick with the fervor of drinks. Words and comments began to surface, fueling tensions, and one jest followed another, each more exacerbated, until opinions clashed inevitably.

A ill-intentioned jest directed at Don Pedro triggered an unexpected turn. Don Pedro insidiously suggested that Benancio's earnings should be shared with the one advising his wife.

- Oh my God, what nonsense! - exclaimed someone amid the confusion. – Goodness gracious! That old man was crazy! Lucky for him, Benancio wasn't carrying his revolver at that moment, or he would've unloaded on him.

However, it took five men to prevent Benancio from beating Don Pedro to death. Pedro was silently led through the back door, while Benancio was restrained in an effort to control the situation, but the determination of the "Bauleño[3]" proved unstoppable. Eventually, he broke free with defiant force. He emerged from the scene with a burning fury, like an unleashed specter. People passing

---

[3] Bauleño, native of the town of El Baúl.

through the main street of the town avoided meeting his gaze, such was the intimidation that emanated from his figure.

The details of what really happened remained shrouded in a veil of mystery. No certainty emerged regarding whether there had been an illicit relationship or not. Versions were varied and scattered. Some whispered that it was an outsider who visited the town for a few days. Others hinted that it could have been Don Pelayo's son. There were even those who speculated that the mayor was involved. Not even the respected priest of the town escaped being dragged into this plot.

According to my father's account, the seed of this intrigue might have been planted by Don Pedro's venomous tongue. Faced with a defeat in a significant bet, Don Pedro could have launched an infamy about Mrs. Gloria. This slander sprang from his thirst for revenge for his own defeat and the trail of bitterness it had left.

Either way, affliction hovered over that defenseless woman, the dedicated teacher who had imparted lessons of the alphabet, numbers, and songs to so many. On that fateful day, the doors of support and protection slammed shut for her. Her cries for help pierced the air and resonated in every corner of the town.

The scene that unfolded was one of immobility and seclusion. The elders, in their desperation, clung to their prayers as if they were a refuge against the turbulent reality. Women cradled their little ones, acting as human shields to shield them from the sight of the tragic scene, refusing to look through window cracks or door crevices. The men fell silent.

House number 5, Benancio's home, a blow echoing on the woman's face.

She embarks on a terrified escape, her pursuer, a man with a knife in hand, relentlessly follows his prey, convinced there is no escape. The woman's tears flow amid her terror as she runs.

The knife's edge finds its target in a first cut, an arm marked by pain, a wound that is not lethal but launches its lament in stabs of agony. The woman falls once again, overcome by panic and pain. In the distance, Madalena and Maria scream but swiftly retreat. "Husband and wife fights, better not to intervene," they whisper as the tumult continues its course.

She falls for the second time. Madalena and Maria scream from afar, but once again, they run. "Husband and wife fights, better not get involved."

The woman gathers strength and heads to the church; old Simón sees her. She falls before reaching the temple, and Simón turns as if nothing had happened.

Second cut, this one to the face. Blood mingles with tears.

As the woman stands up, her steps are unsteady, her resilience gives in to the unrestrained brutality of her assailant. In the heart of this conflict, the hunter delights in chaos and suffering, surrendering to the madness of revenge and unleashed perversity.

At that very moment, in the confines of Pelayo's "pulperia[4]", an eight-year-old boy was present, captivated by the teacher's screams echoing with astonishing bewilderment from the town's main street. This boy was Carmelo, and at that moment, he was immersed in the sweet indulgence of some candies he had acquired with the cents he guarded in his pocket on that sunny day.

Curious and attentive, the boy cautiously peeked through the half-open door of the establishment, and what his eyes captured left an indelible impression on his mind. The figure of Mrs. Gloria approached with difficulty, an image that starkly contrasted with the image he had of his beloved teacher. Her gaze found him, full of sadness and tears, her body covered in blood, transforming the familiar image into a picture of desolation and confusion.

Third cut, the one that killed her. There she fell, and there the boy closed the door on her.

---

4 Pulperia: grocery store

After that fateful episode, Don Benancio made the decision to surrender voluntarily to the town's Civil Chief. It was a swift trial; he admitted his guilt, twenty years in prison. Meanwhile, his young son was taken in by Benancio's sister, who resided in the capital city. In the following years, the destinies of this child and Benancio remained shrouded in mystery, their paths hidden from public view.

Thus, the tragedy unfolded, colored not only by the suffering of Teacher Gloria but also by the shadows it cast over the town. A kind of curse seemed to be cast upon the community, an economic curse that gradually eroded the way of life of its inhabitants, leaving a mark of despair in every corner.

Forty years later, in the cemetery of the town of El Baúl, a man kneels before the neglected and solitary grave of Teacher Gloria. In a gesture of devotion, he crosses himself, and with the passage of time, tears well up. In a sincere plea, he asks for forgiveness and begs for remission, pardon, and possibly mercy. Throughout his life, the memory of Gloria's ghost has tirelessly accompanied him. This man is the boy Carmelo, the one who had the dubious privilege of being the last to see her alive.

The course of this boy, after leaving El Baúl, led him to spend his youth in Arismendi, in the heart of the plains. Later, he faced a significant change by moving to Caracas, a formidable metropolis for him and his family. As he approached his twenties, he became involved in the political movements that emerged in the 1940s and 1950s in the country, advocating for the expansion of democratic rights. During this time, names like "Gallegos, Betancur, Caldera, and Jovito"[5] resonated strongly in the political scene.

He married and had children, presenting himself as an upright and honorable man. However, the memory of his teacher never left him, leaving him with a shadow of guilt. In reality, he had no knowledge of the actual events. Back then, he was just a child.

Once he left the cemetery, his youngest son approached stealthily and whispered in his ear, - Dad, a very beautiful lady told me not to cry anymore, that what happened is in the past, and that you were always her favorite student. Then she kissed me and left. Intrigued, the child asked, – Who is that lady, Dad?

Carmelo looked around, feeling a serenity he had never experienced before. With a radiant smile, he replied, – That lady is forgiveness, kindness, honesty, and patience personified.

---

[5] Politicians who fought for civil rights in Venezuela

¡Chucho! ¡Chucho!

Cojedes State, deep plains, 1927

*"To test reality, we must see it on the tightrope.
When truths become acrobats, we can judge them."*

- Oscar Wilde

In the early 20th century, Venezuela boasted a predominantly rural landscape, marked by virtually nonexistent roads and limited electrical service that barely reached the capital. Faced with this scenario, people held onto the custom of retiring to their homes early and avoiding venturing out once evening fell, all with the purpose of steering clear of being caught by the night in the midst of the vast savannah. It wasn't wise to challenge the possibility of encountering a "tiger butterfly"[6] or venturing down paths inhabited by venomous snakes. Nor was it prudent to tempt fate and run into potential rustlers, ready to take advantage of any opportunity.

It was a country marked by its ruggedness and backwardness, a nation where constant military uprisings and iron-fisted dictatorships prevailed. The visual horizon was dominated by leagues and leagues of dusty roads in the summer and vast expanses of flooded savannah during the winter. It's worth noting that, in those circumstances when the plain was flooded, it happened without delay. I can tell you that I myself have walked through those

---

[6] Leopard

landscapes with water up to my knees for several kilometers, listening to the jingling of rattlesnake bells. It was well-known that being bitten by one of those reptiles would lead to an unfavorable outcome. In such a case, it was preferable for someone to end your suffering with a gunshot.

Nevertheless, caution was not limited solely to rattlesnakes or marsh snakes; in the flooded savannah, the caiman could lurk for its prey, while the anaconda, with its deadly embrace, threatened to break bones. Additionally, the electric eel, whose electric shock was sufficient to dismount a rider, posed a constant danger, with electrocution being a fatal outcome for any individual.

All of this was compounded by the theme of superstitions, apparitions, and ghosts. Moving through the savannah roads at night was akin to an invitation for wandering souls and spirits. In certain cases, these beings even went so far as to negotiate their own salvation, offering burials adorned with gold and "morocotas"[7] in exchange for a prayer or a promise, along with a lit candle in the church of the village.

And so, this narrative begins. It was the time of Holy Week, early April in this case. Don Chucho, a pivotal character in this tale, had received an invitation to attend a celebration at the Guayos estate. Given that Don Chucho was a close friend of

---

[7] Morocota: American gold coin. Colloquial name given in Venezuela.

the estate owner, he did not want to miss the opportunity to enjoy, dance, and drink in the company of acquaintances. Don Chucho, a successful merchant and owner of the most influential "pulperia"[8] in the region, had established his business in El Baúl, in the state of Cojedes. The store was located in his Mansion in the town center, the only Mansion that was also situated by the banks of the El Baúl River. He had his own dock, from where his owned vessels brought goods from Curaçao, Trinidad and Tobago, to be later traded in the central plains and beyond.

Don Chucho was also a family man, having had several children from two marriages, with the first ending due to widowhood, while the second persisted based on his wife's respect for him and under Chucho's firm direction. Though not very docile and proud in character, Don Chucho adhered to solid values. He was a devout Christian and followed the norms of the time. Those who knew him recall that, in the prime of his life, he would look in the mirror near the counter and, with a smile on his face, say to himself:

"What do you lack, Chucho? You have children, you have a beautiful wife, and you have money! What do you lack?"

Returning to the events of interest, I can narrate that the celebration unfolded in an atmosphere of

---

[8] Pulperia: grocery store

camaraderie, and Don Chucho actively participated in the festivities, relishing the company of friends and the local girls who, dressed in their finest attire, sought out prospective suitors. The harp resonated with strength, and the troubadour's voice defied the distance:

- Ahhh lalai lala, The hawk, if it dines, feasts like on livestock it dines.

The voice resonated vigorously in song, stirring the audience with emotion.

- Ah, Carmelito! – exclaimed his friends.

- Today looks like you're gonna hit the jackpot, mate!

They said upon seeing him surrounded by the most beautiful women of the gathering. The hours passed, and the night, with its impenetrable darkness, began to take hold of the surroundings. The sky, gloomy on the horizon, foreshadowed the arrival of somber events. Although Chucho wasn't easily frightened, he felt the need to return home, as early business commitments were calling him.

- Well, this shindig's been great, but it's about time I hit the road and head back to Baul.

Thus, he threw a phrase into the air, as if to make it clear to the diners that he was already leaving.

- Caracha[9], Chucho, with such a pitch-black night, and you're going to take those paths through the hills? You'd be better off staying. I'll give you a hammock so you can spend the night, and tomorrow morning, you can leave at your own pace.

But Chucho replied to the owner of the herd.

- Nope, compadre! I've got business tomorrow, and that can't wait.

No matter how much they tried to convince him with persistence, the man had made up his mind, and nothing and no one could change it. Taking his finely crafted whip, he adjusted his jacket over his elegant "liquiliqui[10]", secured his belt, checked his .38 caliber revolver, adjusted his straw hat, and mounted his mare, beginning his journey. However, before setting off, one of the estate workers warned him:

- Don Chucho, you'd better head through the open plain instead of taking the shortcut through the thicket. There's talk that the ghost of a Spanish soldier who died during the independence days comes out there, and it has given more than a few folks a little spook.

- Ah, Catire[11]! You're quite the cunning one, aren't you, little buddy? You just want to spook me, as if I

---

9 Caracha, Venezuelan expression that refers to some complicated situation.
10 typical Venezuelan costume.
11 Catire: blond

were a greenhorn falling for those tricks. Those are just tales, roadside stories meant to scare husbands who live from one shindig to another, - Chucho replied with determination.

- Look, Don Chucho, I've got a lot of respect for you to be messing around like that, sir. I'm just telling you what more than a few folks have seen around these parts, and I'm telling you it's no joke. For real, Don Chucho, for real! - The young man insisted, sincerity evident in his words.

Interrupting the thread of the story, I want to point out that "ánimas" refers to the souls of those who have died and, due to their sins, are confined to purgatory—a fearsome place where, surrounded by fire and suffering, they must wait until the stain of their sins disappears and they become worthy of ascending to paradise. To achieve this purification, souls must be in constant prayer, seeking forgiveness from God.

The word "ánima" comes from Latin: anima, and can be translated as breath, air, or vital principle. In ancient times, it was believed that the soul was connected to the breath or breath that God had placed in humans to animate them. Therefore, "ánima" is the soul of humans. From there, this word passed into Spanish as a synonym for soul but also for a wandering soul.

Continuing with the story, we find that Chucho let out a hearty laugh and, mounting his mare, uttered a phrase into the air that harked back to ancient times.

- With God!!!

With the preparations complete, Chucho embarked on his journey. The path to the town would take at least an hour if he chose the route through the thicket. This thicket, a vast island of trees in the midst of the savannah, was traversed by a spring whose current served as a guide for travelers. Trying to go around this area would add an extra 30 to 40 minutes to the journey, and Chucho wanted to return early to get some rest before facing his workday the next morning.

Upon reaching the threshold of the mentioned forest, Chucho recalled the words of the estate worker with a touch of irony and whispered to himself:

- Who are we going with?

- With God.

He answered himself, then added:

- And with the Virgin.

Having said this, he entered the grove, and the darkness of the tree canopy enveloped him completely. The echo of the horse's hooves resonated with an ominous echo as Chucho advanced through the thicket of forests rising from the edge of the savannah. The dancing shadows of twisted branches seemed to whisper dark secrets, and the leaves rustled like whispers of past sorrows. As he delved deeper into the tangled maze of twisted trees, the wind began to carry a distant murmur. It was a murmur that echoed with an anguished echo, whispers of his name, an insistent calling that began to disturb him.

- Chu-cho, Chu-cho

His ears picked up a call that seemed to emanate from something non-human. To regain his composure, he decided to raise his voice and spoke firmly:

- What a merry mucker, always foolin' around! And the ghost of a Spanish soldier? That's just playin' tricks!

However, before completing the statement, the grating murmur made itself present again, repeating his name in the darkness.

- Chu-cho, Chu-cho...

This compelled him to halt his mount, and, filled with distrust, he gripped his Coleman lantern—a product he traded quite well in those parts—trying to illuminate in all directions in search of the origin of that call. Every time he thought he had pinpointed the direction of the voice, it shifted, quickening the pace of his heart. The dense twilight and the feeling that something lurked from the shadows filled him with apprehension. Amidst the uncertainty, he took a crucifix given to him by his second wife and, clutching it tightly, desperately searched through the thick foliage. However, the source of the call remained elusive, and the conviction that something unknown was watching him heightened his unease.

Once more, he uttered a prayer into the air, this time laden with a threat:

- Who's there? Look, I don't mess around. I've got my revolver, and if you're playing games, I'll shoot you.

Not long after delivering the harangue, once again and defiantly, the call echoed from the shadows.

- Chu-cho, Chu-cho...

The man resumed his march, for, like any good llanero, he was not one to turn his back on danger. However, the apprehension of not knowing who or what was calling him lingered. What was clear, though, was that as he advanced, the tone of the call intensified. Although the other sounds of the forest and the breeze weaving through the trees intermingled, making it challenging for him to pinpoint the precise source of this phenomenon.

Immersed in this situation, with the night closing in and the drizzle hinting at an impending storm, Don Chucho had remarkably maintained his calm. However, his composure was disrupted when a lightning bolt, striking nearby, split a tree in the shape of a cross, igniting a small fire and causing a detonation that echoed like the roar of a German cannon from 1914. The horse's reaction to the blast resulted in a frenzy that threw the rider to the ground. In that instant, Chucho found himself alone in the middle of the forest, without his mount, as the rain intensified and that mysterious apparition continued invoking his name incessantly.

Chucho quickly rose from the ground, brandishing his revolver as he walked on foot among the trees. At that very moment, the storm intensified: the wind blew forcefully, rain pierced through the dense foliage, and lightning illuminated the darkness of the night. To make matters worse, the situation with the unknown caller increased in both quantity and speed:

- Chu-cho!, Chu-cho!, Chu-cho!, Chu-cho!, Chu-cho!, Chu-cho!

It wasn't just the quantity but the speed of the call that was faster. It was as if the specter or whatever it was that addressed him synchronized with the violence of the storm.

Receiving no response other than that relentless call, Chucho fired his revolver in various directions, as if trying to harm anything responsible for calling him insistently. Instead, this action seemed to unleash the hatred of the manifestation. Additionally, the rain and wind heightened their force, and the calling intensified in both continuity and speed:

- Chu-cho!, Chu-cho!, Chu-cho!, Chu-cho!, Chu-cho!, Chu-cho!

There comes a point in a man's life when, feeling cornered and with no options, he insists on confronting the evil that threatens him. In Chucho's case, this was no exception. He moved, keeping the revolver with him, determined to face this unknown evil with his life if necessary. As he advanced, the calling became more intense in its resonance. What was clear at that moment was that, whatever it was, it was above him, looking down from the treetops. Then, a new lightning bolt illuminated the area, and the man's face showed a strong impression, releasing a loud scream that turned into laughter resembling the laughter of a madman:

- Ahhhhhhhh, hahahahahahahahaha!

- Hail Mary Most Pure, conceived without sin.

He said with force, then he dropped to the ground, like a soldier who, after finishing a battle, surrenders to fatigue when adrenaline no longer propels him into the fight.

The fact was that, as he raised his gaze, Chucho noticed at the exact moment the lightning illuminated the trees that a branch was moving in the direction of the wind. This branch, brushing against a natural fork that had formed in a mango bush, created the sound "Chu," and due to the physical effect of the same branch springing back, it produced the other sound, "Cho." Although the sound might not have been exactly like his name "Chucho," the suggestion initiated by the estate worker and the intensity of the atmospheric conditions of the night caused our protagonist's brain to interpret it as the call to his name.

After this, the "Don" walked out of the thicket to see that his mount was waiting for him, grazing in the savannah. He took his horse and returned to the town, and days later, his story was circulating from mouth to mouth among the people in those parts.

Witches like salt

Tinaco[12], Cojedes State, 1962.

"Do not judge anything by its appearance, but by the evidence. There is no better rule."

- Charles Dickens

In the psyche of the children from my homeland, an instinctive fear is deeply rooted when it comes to the image of witches. These beings might be summoned through the well-known phrase used by mothers and grandmothers: "If you don't behave, the witch will come for you." All of this is employed as a means of coercion when children resist embracing the path of good behavior. The constant repetition of this expression generates intense fear, as if it were a natural enemy of the little ones. The witch is like the cat, and the child is the mouse.

It is known among the children of the Venezuelan plains that witches are malevolent entities, usually depicted as women, their figures bent under the weight of age and wickedness. They are attributed the ability to transform into any animal, but above all, to shrink in size to slip through the cracks of adobe homes and search for children in their rooms. Similar to the image of the European vampire, these witches would suck the blood of their victims,

---

[12] Tinaco is a town in rural areas of Venezuela

showing a preference for toe fingers to sink their fangs into. It is said that the younger the child, the more tender, the more appetizing and desired by this demon.

With this introduction, I want to share a story that everyone discussed in my grandmother's old colonial house, and I want to make it clear that everyone I've spoken to swears that the events I'm about to narrate happened exactly as described. According to the stories circulating, this event took place in the house located just across the street. I will forever be indebted to the owner of that place because, in a separate chapter of my childhood, she bravely defended my life against a man who, armed with a pistol, attempted to end my existence. The reason behind this attack attempt was that, due to boys' games, I made the man fall off his motorcycle by losing balance because of a skateboard that slipped from my feet. It wasn't premeditated; it had been an accident. The man got up with the intention of shooting me with the weapon he carried, but that old lady was braver than the bravest of males, and while she may have been humble in wealth, she had an abundance of courage.

Thus, this anecdote not only highlights the shared history in my grandmother's colonial house but also demonstrates how courage can manifest in the most unexpected and powerful ways.

The rum flowed abundantly, and the appetizers were equally generous. The atmosphere was saturated with the melodies of the plains, and occasionally, the notes of "Billo's Caracas Boys[13]" slipped in, providing an opportunity for the young ones to dance. Everything was proceeding perfectly in this scene that I'm trying to describe to you. However, amid this festive backdrop, there was an episode going unnoticed by everyone.

Francisco had decided to distance himself from the center of the party, venturing into the backyard where the lights didn't reach with their full intensity. Taking advantage of the crowd's attention being captured by the general merriment, he sought out Marina in the shadows, near the chicken coop at the back. Good Lord. Right in the midst of the celebration, and Francisco couldn't restrain himself.

The Bible, in Exodus 20:17, teaches us: "You shall not covet your neighbor's house; you shall not covet your neighbor's wife, nor his male servant, nor his female servant, nor his ox, nor his donkey, nor anything that is your neighbor's." In my understanding, it's also valid to add that one should not covet another person's spouse, as such desires can inflict irreparable wounds on individuals. Clearly, this principle did not apply to Marina, and she reveled in every available pleasure. The way

---

[13] Very popular music band in Venezuela and Colombia between 1950 and 1980

Marina embraced life was notably different. She delighted in the availability of the moment, and her focus did not pause for social or moral conventions. It seemed that coveting any pleasure that crossed her path was her norm. This reckless approach, while satisfying in the moment, had repercussions that couldn't be ignored, especially when other hearts became entangled in the process. Her lifestyle, fueled by impulses, starkly contrasted with the deeper values dictated by morality.

About 20 minutes passed, and as Laura didn't see her husband, a certain degree of concern crept in, prompting her to roam around the house. In one of the rooms, she observed the babies of one of the daughters of the lady, an 8-month-old and a 3-year-old girl. They were snugly tucked in a crib, covered with a mosquito net to shield them from any pests. Additionally, the soft hum of the table fan came to life. With a constant and soothing rhythm, the device swayed from left to right, creating a cool breeze that caressed the skin. The 'shhhhhh' sound mixed with the gentle mechanical murmur, filling the space with a sense of comfort and tranquility. Intrigued by these elements, Laura approached to observe them closely. As she gazed upon the scene, her mind projected a familiar image: the vision of her own children, who should be sleeping peacefully at her grandmother's house at that moment.

Laura continued wandering through the house and finally felt compelled to head towards the back of the yard, where the chicken coop was situated. At that moment, the moans of a woman captured her attention, as if life itself were narrating a chapter she was not meant to witness. The phrase "Out of sight, out of mind" echoed in her head, but like Lot's wife, who turned into salt for yielding to her curiosity, Laura also experienced a similar shock. Her heart, in turn, turned into salt as she confirmed the truth her reluctant eyes couldn't deny: the woman moaning was Marina, and the man sharing that moment with her was her own husband, Francisco.

If Laura had resisted the temptation to uncover the culprits behind those moans, Francisco would have returned to her side minutes later, offering any excuse to calm the turbulent waters. However, destiny had other plans. The image Laura could never erase from her mind was that of Marina and Francisco, hidden behind the fence surrounding the chicken coop. But what was even more devastating for Laura was the way Marina looked at her boldly when their eyes met, as if shame were not an obstacle but a triviality in the face of the opportunity to be observed.

In an instant, Laura's life took an unforeseen turn, confronting her with the painful reality of betrayal and deceit. The yard, once a place of serenity and refuge, transformed into the stage for a silent and cruel confession.

Due to her conciliatory nature and her status as a lady, Laura chose not to unleash a scandal amid the celebration. With eyes blurred by tears but maintaining unwavering dignity, she discreetly withdrew to find a space where she could gather her thoughts. With determination, she dried her tears and returned to the gathering, but her participation was marked by a palpable distance and a lack of connection with her surroundings. Although physically present, her mind wandered in a whirlwind of emotions and unanswered questions.

Shortly after, Francisco returned to the scene, straightening his guayabera and placing a kiss on Laura's cheek. For her, that gesture, which used to be comforting, turned into a stabbing sensation, like sharp knives piercing her heart. As she watched his return, her thoughts became a mix of confusion and pain, unable to find an appropriate response to confront the betrayal she had witnessed.

Marina, on the other hand, did not return to the event. Perhaps she needed time to compose herself, both emotionally and in terms of her physical appearance. Or maybe, amidst the internal storm of remorse or fear, she chose to keep her distance, avoiding any direct confrontation with Laura. Perhaps she wanted to prevent a potential public confrontation with Laura, which could expose the uncomfortable truth to everyone present. At that moment, Marina's silence seemed both a measure of self-protection and a way to prevent her mistake from becoming even more evident.

It was 3 in the morning, and in the midst of this whirlwind of events, the typical custom of the elders in the area emerged, initiating their tales of spooks and apparitions. In the midst of these narratives, the story of witches could not be missing. It was at that precise moment when one of the attendees, clearly affected by alcohol, interrupted the storytelling with a sarcastic tone:

- Blimey! Witches ain't real, it's all a bleedin' tale. The only witches I know are them birds I've shagged.

This comment initially elicited silence, followed by laughter that spread among those present.

- Blimey, Perucho! You're proper bladdered, and it's only 3 in the bleedin' morning.

Responded one of his friends with a conspiratorial tone.

However, he hadn't finished uttering his response when a black, voluminous shadow fluttered over the house, moving with the agility of a predator in search of its prey. Dogs went mad, barking incessantly, birds were startled from their slumber, filling the air with their cries, while chickens in the coop cackled as if emitting cries of distress. A repugnant odor filled the air, and the lights inside the house began to flicker. The being or entity was so immense that it even obscured the twinkle of the stars, plunging the sky into an even deeper darkness. Someone in the assembly commented:

-   Look at that vulture! What a huge creature!

But those who live in the rural areas know that vultures do not fly at night, or at least it's not their custom. They have adapted to fly and feed during the day, and they seek places where there is carrion, and the presence of the noise of a party would scare them away.

-   That is not a vulture! – exclaimed the elderly servant, who was in charge of caring for the children in the house. At the same time, she signaled to the mother of the babies (mentioned in paragraphs above) to go check on their well-being in their room, with the assistance of other women and some men from the house. The other children still awake sought refuge in the arms of their mothers, while the elders crossed themselves in an act of spiritual protection.

Next, the maid went to the kitchen and grabbed a handful of salt. After making a cross in the center of the courtyard, she exclaimed firmly:

-   Hail Mary, full of grace. I sanctify this house with the power of God so that you never set foot in this place again. And come tomorrow for salt, witch of hell.

After this act, a scream echoed, and the creature or whatever it was lost control, colliding with a branch of the tree. The branch broke, falling a bit lower, taking the perfect shape of a cross. Immediately after, the presence fled into the darkness of the night, restoring calm. The scene of the woman's fierce spiritual struggle against the apparition left everyone, even the bravest men, with trembling legs. But you might wonder, why did the old woman challenge it to come back for salt the next day? Well, it is known that salt attracts witches, and it is the best way to discover if a witch dwells among the people of a community.

The event left such a profound impression that the attendees began to quickly bid farewell to the hosts of the house, eager to return to their own homes. That night, children and young people from the entire locality slept in the same rooms as their parents, which had been adorned with crosses made from sanctified palm to prevent any malevolent entity from entering their spaces.

With the new day came the crowing of the rooster, the chant that announced the apostle Peter's betrayal, and along with it, the chorus of birds rose, chasing away the nocturnal ghosts that typically haunted children. It was the sweetest moment to take advantage of and enjoy restful sleep, leaving behind the fears of the previous night. In the house where the party had taken place, while preparing arepas[14], a young woman entered the kitchen with a surprising message: there was a woman outside requesting a bit of salt, as she had run out at her home. Everyone was perplexed by this news, but the experienced servant took some salt from the kitchen and headed towards the door, where she found Marina waiting shyly and hesitant to set foot inside. The servant looked her in the eyes and handed her the salt, at that moment, Marina walked down the street, disappearing from the town never to return again.

---

[14] Arepa is a typical Venezuelan food made from corn flour.

Ermenegilda de Núñez

Tinaco, Cojedes State, 1942

"Not to be loved is a simple misfortune; the true misfortune is not to love."

- Albert Camus

I'm not sure how to approach this story. I don't know if it's about an apparition, a family, or the house where this family lived. Maybe it's a mix of everything. This is an account of a series of events that intertwine the living and the dead, love and heartbreak, the successes and mistakes that mark people's existence.

Let's begin by exploring the dwelling. A colonial mansion that housed my grandmother, or I could say my aunt Lina, or if we step back even further in time, it belonged to Colonel Núñez and his wife Ermenegilda, and who knows who else if we delve deeper into the past. The truth is that this house triggered in me a concert of conflicting emotions.

During the day, it exuded a sense of peace and tranquility. Its cool corridors were usually open to a beautiful inner courtyard, surrounded by lush orange and mango trees whose branches provided shelter against the harsh llanero sun, creating a natural air conditioning. Along the walls of the courtyard, there were jasmine vines that climbed the walls, creating a palette of vibrant colors with their pink, red, and white flowers. These plants added a sense of freshness and life to the surroundings, as well as providing shade and a respite from the scorching sun.

The courtyard floor was paved with stone pavers or terracotta slabs, arranged in a geometric design that evoked a more Islamic-Spanish heritage. This design helped to trace a path within the courtyard that was surrounded by white stones amidst the soil that also covered most of the land. Over time, however, I have to mention that the corridors were barred to protect the inhabitants from the insecurity that prevailed in the streets. And the patio area was covered with an ugly white concrete that did not have the same style that I enjoyed as a child. The "advantages" of modern times, as they would say, what irony.

At the entrance of the house, there was not a simple door, but a gate. A monumental colonial gate, built with solid wood, which at night was secured with a horizontal iron bar. It resembled the gate of a medieval castle, but instead of stopping an English knight like Ivanhoe, it was designed to keep at bay the hordes of rebels that ravaged Venezuela in the late 19th century.

Continuing the narrative, if you followed the corridor to your left upon entering the place, you would come across my grandmother's room. It was a cozy space where my grandmother rested on one bed, while my aunt Lina slept on the other. My grandmother's bed was positioned next to the bay window, or rather, the grand bay window. A bay window was a generous opening that evoked the romance of bygone times, where young women were imagined sitting on one of the inner edges, waiting to be captivated by a serenade. Reality, of course, tended to be more harsh and melancholic, although there was always the possibility of giving it a dreamlike touch.

The windows of colonial houses cannot simply be called "windows"; that would be almost a euphemism. Their design is distinctive: ornate, with bars, large, long, and low, with an inner sill where ladies sat to observe the street through the bars that kept them as if they were captives. Captives of the sin of being touched, like odalisques in a sultan's harem. Above the upper external sill, a projecting "hat" is placed, known as "coronela," preferably light and generally made of adobe or plaster.

Latin American windows are a multicolored symphony and lack a standard design, contributing to the towns of our land appearing immersed in a perpetual carnival of colors. Very different from North American towns, steeped in the cold and darkness of their gray and somber hues. This description would likely be disturbing to the Austrian architect Adolf Loos, a staunch opponent of the excesses of the Baroque and classical architecture with its ornaments and bas-reliefs.

In his writings, he left the following statement: "Flee from America, for a ghost haunts it from Iberia. Among the Trujillanos[15], he found devotees of immeasurable delight. They are so devoted that they have more than 300 idols in their city of no more than 60 blocks. It is not enough for them to stain their facades with their sin, like the Jews in Egypt with the blood of the lamb, but they hang these images inside their homes and scatter them throughout the world." Too Germanic for my taste.

Continuing with the description of the residence, turning to the right from the entrance corridor, we encounter a wall full of memories where a sword that could date back to the time of Venezuelan independence and some old spurs are embedded in rather rustic frames. Just below this, there was my Uncle Rene's organ. My uncle had entered the seminary with the intention of becoming a priest, but he never completed his training. He had started a restaurant business, but soon grew bored of it. He had tried various things, but it seemed that the diligence and discipline of a worker were not his best qualities. However, he possessed notable education and creativity. His drawings exuded considerable beauty, and his mastery of the organ was appreciated by those who enjoyed it. But, as I mentioned, his main challenge seemed to be the inability to bring his projects to fruition. I'm not sure if this was due to innate laziness or a lack of

---

[15] Native of the city of Trujillo

determination to face life; nevertheless, his education and cultural wealth were highly respectable.

Another distinctive trait of my uncle was his ability to dress with elegance and style, something that always impressed me and contrasted with my own tendency to wear whatever garment is available.

Continuing in that direction and to the right, there was a spacious room that could well be described as an internal hall. It used to be the place where I had to sleep when I visited the house, and there I spent some of the most distressing nights of my life. It was said that Ermenegilda's ghost appeared in this room, a mystery I will discuss later. Furthermore, to complicate things even more, an ancient weapons burial was discovered in this room, which my grandfather decided to re-bury for fear that the current government would use them as evidence of an attempted uprising. Above this place, I never knew exactly where, but I deduce it was in the center, where there was a drawing of a star with its circle. I must admit that this star made me feel uneasy, although its design was probably just an aesthetic choice by the floor's builder. Additionally, there were large, antique wardrobes that terrified me, largely due to the maids' stories, claiming that a hairy hand would reach out from there to grab my feet during the night. Day or night, the truth is that I didn't like being in that room.

Further down the hallway, there was my uncle's room. A long and narrow room with a hammock at the entrance and a double bed at the end. Opposite the window, and this was a more modern window, was my uncle's library. What a library he had! Who knows where all those wonderful books ended up. There were works by Quevedo, Lope de Vega, Cervantes, Schopenhauer, Rómulo Gallegos, Kafka, Dante, Victor Hugo, world history, religion, science, and art. There was everything, even books that could be over 200 years old. Perhaps my uncle was born into the wrong family and in the wrong place.

I continue the tour, this time turning left from my uncle's room, and we find ourselves in the dining room. During celebrations, the dining room was filled with the best foods and drinks one could imagine. Sometimes, the dining table was covered with a brightly colored tablecloth. A blend of Spanish and Venezuelan Creole cuisine could be found, with Iberian ham, chorizo, and salchichón[16] emanating an irresistible aroma, accompanied by olives and local white cheese that melted in the mouth. All of this was complemented by the hallaca[17] and Venezuelan ham bread.

After the dining room, you would come across the kitchen. It was a very rustic place, but over time, it

---

[16] sausage
[17] typical Venezuelan food

was renovated to have a more modern look. My grandmother was always there, as she was a very hardworking woman. Life didn't give her many choices, and her personality wouldn't have led her down a different path either. She was an Italian who probably arrived in Venezuela in the early 20th century with her entire family and married at a somewhat advanced age for the standards of the time because her parents disapproved of my grandfather's skin tone. My grandmother had brown hair, was very fair, and extremely beautiful, while my grandfather was black and a poet, also a schoolteacher. My grandmother was a practical and not very affectionate woman; my grandfather, as described by my mother, was a tender but very dreamy man. I'll talk a little more about this relationship later, but for now, let's continue with the house review.

If you continued further, you would end up exiting the kitchen into what was originally a small backyard that culminated in a wattle wall, and nearby there was a semeruco or cherry tree. In Venezuela, semeruco is known as "cerecita," but the local fruit has an unparalleled flavor. As Luis Mariano Rivera aptly expressed:

"Cherry from my mountain,

Sweet and pure little fruit,

Tangy from my sky

And from my land, sweetness to suit."

Years later, that tree died of old age and was cut down. In its place, an entrance was constructed to use it as a garage, which always saddened me because I knew I would never taste a fruit with such flavor again, and many good memories died along with that tree.

To conclude, from that small backyard, there was an entrance leading to the main courtyard I mentioned earlier. From there, it connected to the chicken coop and the space where the tortoises were kept. In Venezuela, a cake is prepared with tortoise meat, a practice I personally dislike due to the way these poor animals are sacrificed. Additionally, when I was a child, I had a tortoise as a pet, so it's not easy for me to consider eating one, even though I'm not a vegan or anything like that.

Another thing I want to mention is that in the main courtyard, there was a kind of "caney[18]," although it wasn't made of thatched or palm leaf roof, it was an open-sided shed supported by metal beams but reminiscent of the concept of a caney. There, we would sit in the evenings to discuss teenage things, occasionally flirt with some girls my age, or simply throw stones at anything passing by just for the sake of annoying each other. There, too, we would hear ghost stories originating from the experiences of the maids or house helpers.

---

[18] Shed with a palm or straw roof, without walls and supported by forks.

Having sketched the outline of the colonial house, I now long to weave some words around the souls that occupied it. In the town records, the construction was dated around 1800. It is said that Ignacio Núñez, a colonel according to the family saga, was the original owner. However, this claim cannot be asserted with absolute certainty. In the chronicles, the name of his wife, Ermenegilda or perhaps Hermenegilda, intertwines in an ambiguity that challenges certainty. Nevertheless, allowing the wind of speculation to flutter the curtains of time, I testify that this couple lived through one of the darkest chapters in Venezuela's chronicle.

The dawn of independence in 1810 looms large in memory, crossing the thresholds of the conflict that would swell the years until 1821. An era in which destinies twisted, and calamities were woven with strands of fury. The 19th century, in its sorrow, threw upon the shoulders of Venezuelans the burden of survival, a task they undertook after the turmoil of war. The federal war, which erupted twenty years later, solidified its scythe over the already shattered hopes.

A well-known figure of the time, General Boves[19], painted the country's history with blood and fire between 1811 and 1813, and his deeds may or may not have crossed the threshold of Tinaco, the town where this story unfolds. Although I omit such

---

[19] Spanish soldier

details, as he doesn't even deserve my mention to lean towards his figure. He, who fervently embodied the purest manifestation of iniquity and terror. The possibility remains that others, with a slightly different nuance, have marched through the shadows, indistinguishable from the terrible general.

The conflict was so ruthless that even falling into the hands of the independence forces did not provide substantial respite. With caution, I will weave the narrative of one of the many incidents that bloodied the land, one of the acts that painted darkness onto the epic of Boves and his legions:

...Having triumphed in Calabozo, Boves' forces invaded towns and villages, giving rise to new factions. They murdered anyone they deemed patriots, especially if they possessed any valuables to plunder. What they couldn't take, they destroyed. Each acted according to their most perverse inclinations, killing without restraint, and there was no commander to stop them; rather, Boves took pleasure in pillaging. When Boves was present, they forcibly brought forward the elderly, women, and children, demanding their heads. The criminal usually granted this request, and the victims perished by spear or were dragged by the horses' tails, a source of amusement. These barbarians violated women and girls, then either whipped them or took their lives when they were not kept for further abuse...

How many tormented souls must there be in that country? How many ghosts roam that territory, carrying the pain of a life marked by curses? Venezuela has endured 200 years of tragedies, including tyrants, coups, and revolutions that never seem to end, one following the other. Could it be that we bear a curse for the atrocities committed in those times? Because, if we consider, even though Boves was Spanish, his troops were quite "criollitas[20]", meaning that this wickedness was carried out brother against brother.

How much could Tinaco have suffered? I cannot assert it, but it was very likely touched in some way by that maelstrom. This was the scenario that Colonel Ignacio Núñez had to face, and it could have been the origin of the weapons that were found buried in the living room of the house more than a century later. "What more can I discover about this couple? My attempts to obtain information from the town records were futile. The only clue I have is that the house later came into the possession of an individual named Mirabal, although I lack details on this matter.

Later, the property changed hands and came under the administration of my grandfather. I have records that in 1927, he married my grandmother, although I cannot definitively state whether their first residence was precisely that house or another.

---

[20] Criollo: creole, native, vernacular

Ultimately, it is with my grandparents that this narrative gains vision and depth, so I will take some time to outline their stories as detailed as possible.

Let me begin with my grandmother, Feliciana Fiori. She arrived in Venezuelan lands with her family when she was still an infant, although there is a legend that her birth occurred in the very bowels of a ship. This matter is not for me to confirm; what I am sure of is that her roots traced back to Naples. In particular, I once glimpsed the birth certificate of one of my great-grandparents, a relic that confirmed the Neapolitan origin. I picture this group of beings venturing into the rural stage of the early 20th century, resisting the onslaught of the relentless heat that characterizes the Venezuelan plains. Overflowing rivers inhabited by piranhas and alligators, and vast expanses of plains dotted with shrubbery. Months of torrential rains followed by scorching months when the sun punishes without mercy. I do not know the exact paths that brought them to this town in the central plains, but it is known that my great-grandfather carved out a prosperous path within the community, amassing a certain fortune.

Of my grandmother, I retain memories of her later years. I was never very close to her; she was not a very affectionate woman, at least not with me. I can't say she was a bad grandmother, but the kind of warmth that other women have with their grandchildren was not present. Although I mentioned her old age, I assert with certainty that, in her youth, she possessed striking beauty. Her face, in days gone by, must have been an exquisite marvel, and her body, slender but carefully sculpted. I also know, in addition, that this lady was an active woman, owner of her own ventures, such as a bakery that nourished the entire community amidst the plague that ravaged the town in times long past. Moreover, she was always involved in plans to support the family. She represents an archetype of her time, a woman who had no time to be depressed over trivialities, an indefatigable fighter who refused to succumb to the onslaughts of life, even in the face of the countless challenges imposed by the nation's difficulties and my grandfather's modest salary. Perhaps, precisely for this reason, she did not have the space for typical grandmotherly indulgences.

I understand that Feliciana, at a very young age, was involved in a romance or, at least, was courted by a young man from a respectable family in the same town. However, these romantic involvements were disapproved by Feliciana's parents because the young man was afflicted with tuberculosis, and at that time, the disease carried a stigma. The relationship took on tragic hues because the young man ultimately succumbed to the illness, deeply affecting my grandmother. They say in the town that during the wake, the deceased's eyes remained open, and no one could close them until my grandmother decided to go to the place to offer her condolences. As she approached the deceased, he closed his eyes without any explanation. The grieving mother embraced my grandmother and whispered, "He has finally found peace." This must have been very sad for my grandmother because if she had any hopes of establishing a relationship with that man, providence imposed its wishes over hers. My sisters recount that perhaps that young man could have been the love of my grandmother's life. However, higher powers acted with their own will, charting a divergent course for her destiny. Thus, she was forced to content herself with mere presence at the wake, as permission to attend the burial was denied. It is said that she observed the funeral procession from the seclusion of her window, a distance that, despite being physical, spiritually separated her from that farewell she could never utter. Years later, this scene brought to me a verse that describes the tragedy of that unfinished relationship.

"I'm not afraid of death,

I'm afraid of sin

The sin of forgetting you

And you forgetting me."

In the other corner of this tale, my grandfather emerges. He first saw the light in Manrique, in the parish of San Carlos municipality. However, at the age of twelve, life's currents cast him into the domains of Tinaco. He was an unrecognized son, but Ángel María Garrido, a martyr in the battle against dictator Juan Vicente Gómez, played a paternal role in his life. I know that the remains of Ángel María rest in the Tinaco cemetery; alongside the grave, you'll find the shackles from the cells of Gómez's regime that persisted until his death.

The mother who brought him into the world answered to the name Eliana, although her existence faded away when he was barely three years old. It is said that Eliana had a fair face and blue eyes, but she was undone by a man whom my lips refuse to name, as he does not deserve a place in this story – a sort of modern chieftain who claimed everything in the area, and from whom my grandfather inherited his dark complexion.

To proceed on this journey, I emphasize that my grandfather carried the darkness in his skin, his slender figure, and his calm and tranquil demeanor. Nevertheless, he undoubtedly inherited from Ángel María the rebellious passion for freedom. In his full adulthood, police precincts harbored his figure on numerous occasions due to dissenting opinions against the yokes of dictatorial regimes.

This conduct, probably, did not generate gratitude in my grandmother. With eight children making their entrance into life, the responsibility of supporting the household fell on the Italian woman, who demonstrated notable skill with her culinary business and kept the family afloat for years. I highlight that my grandfather embraced literature, even with scarce resources. With perseverance and determination, he delved into philosophy and literature, revealing himself as a poet and teacher. His verses won prizes and awards, and in 1934, the French government awarded him a diploma and medal after winning the literary contest sponsored by that country with his masterful "Song to France." My mother used to tell me that poverty was such that my grandfather wrote his poems in the blank margins of regional newspapers. I regret not having had the pleasure of meeting him.

The union of my grandparents was sealed in 1927; however, an unofficial commitment extended for seven years before their formal bond. My grandmother's family did not bless the union because of my grandfather's dark skin, which they disapproved of in their daughter's marriage. The exact intricacies of their relationship elude me, but two anecdotes guide me. The first, the primary reason for this narrative, lies in the fact that my grandfather slept in the living room, the same room I outlined in the opening lines. A place that, I confess, carried a certain unsettling aura for me. The circumstance of my grandmother displacing him from the bedroom they shared, after some dispute whose nature I do not know, sheds light on this event. The second episode, years later, in the postmortem era of my grandfather, when my grandmother visited Caracas and strolled with my sister along the Boulevard de Sabana Grande, the anecdote comes to life. My sister, referring to that moment, recounts how my grandmother, in a burst of melancholy, stopped in front of a clothing store with a gaze that exuded sorrow and, in a hushed whisper, uttered the words: "If I were to be born again, I wouldn't get married again." I have a theory that some people are born never to be happy, and I believe my grandmother was one of them.

In addition to the central figures, two additional protagonists stand out in this journey: my aunt Lina and my uncle Rene, of whom I have already outlined and detailed certain lines. It is only fair to mention that my grandparents brought eight offspring into the world; however, only my uncle Rene and my aunt Lina established a constant residence in that dwelling. Since the focus of this narrative revolves around the inhabitants, I have decided to respect the margin of mentions for the rest of the family.

After sketching Rene's profile, I now turn my narrative to Lina. Oh, Aunt Lina! What a singular character! My attempt to capture her essence in words faces a challenge that I do not underestimate, but I will strive to portray her as faithfully as possible. Interweaving her features into the palette of my narration is an ambitious goal; with humility and respect, I venture into it.

Lina, the youngest daughter, exhibited a distinct physiognomy. Her features, not so closely tied to the Italian traits of my grandmother, rather resembled the creole features with hints of indigenous hues. Her straight black hair, as dark as jet, adorned her figure of modest stature, a proportional and pleasing body to the eye. She was not ugly. Her way of expressing herself, typically plainspoken, transcended to the point that her nephews, in play and affection, emulated her style, and she seemed unfazed by it. Matrimony found no place in her life. I am not clear on whether suitors or relationships crossed her path, but I do know that she inherited from my grandmother a hardworking tenacity and a survival-oriented proactivity. Unlike my grandmother, who carved her path in commerce, Lina, like a beacon of determination, directed her steps towards education, and this is where my admiration for her lies. For years, she took a daily bus from Tinaco to the city of Valencia, where she immersed herself in her law studies. Beyond obtaining her law degree, her achievements reached the position of judge in the state of Cojedes. A tireless worker, undoubtedly.

But, like a whirlwind of emotions and nuances, Lina embodied a complex character. Her temperament swung on the thin line between friend and antagonist. She was one of those souls who, once on your side, provided unconditional help; but, in a scenario of discord, unleashed a fury that could be compared to the burning of Troy. A creature of an intensity that, in the local parlance, is called "venático" and which, in modern times influenced by foreign nomenclature, is labeled as "bipolar." However, we do not refer to the "bipolar" concept rooted in northern lands, where pills are the answer to existential confusion. We speak of the "bipolar" of these Latin American lands, which, with frankness and rawness, expresses discontent without considering to whom it is directed. In short, Lina did not pause for the subtleties of diplomacy. Her lack of diplomacy, however, spawned discord in her relationship with my grandmother, as the factions engaged in fierce battles over any trivial matter. The intertwined personalities of my grandmother and Lina wove an unavoidable conflict.

Having painted the background with as much detail as possible, I now delve into the unsettling mysteries that embrace my grandmother's ancient colonial dwelling. I refuse to entangle myself in the web of scientific or sociological explanations feasible for such cases, choosing instead the simple act of narrating these stories. Multiple tales interweave their enigma, some perhaps even hidden in the shadows of the unknown.

The first episode that emerges from the corner of my memory dates back to the early days of my grandparents' marriage. In those nascent years, my mother was still a small creature. As I mentioned earlier in the narrative, discord stirred the marital nest, relegating my grandfather to sleep in the vastness of the grand living room. My grandfather proceeded to hang his hammock over the floor where a black star is now painted, preparing to endure what I imagine was not a good moment for him. Allow me to doubt that such a star stood there at that time.

Captivated by the weight of the argument, my grandfather sank into the arms of sleep, but around three in the morning, he was awakened by the chilling sensation of a scrutinizing presence watching him from the shadows. Cold breath escaped from his lips into the warm Tinaco night, an anomaly that did not go unnoticed. His gaze met a figure shrouded in white, gliding toward him, oblivious to the time of his reality.

Shadows! Shadows! Shadows! The white lady is coming for you.

Having adapted his vision to the darkness, my ancestor could discern that it was a woman, dressed in attire unfamiliar to the era in which my grandfather found himself, with a hairstyle well past its fashion. To delve into more detail, she was a lady with a round but pretty face, her black hair elegantly gathered in a bun or elaborate hairstyle, allowing some curls and loose strands that framed her face. Accessories like combs or headbands were part of this presentation. The dress was made of very fine fabric, perhaps silk, satin, or lace, and featured a high and tight waist.

"Shadows! Shadows! Shadows! The white lady is coming for you."

Fearing to have crossed the border between dreams and wakefulness, my grandfather inquired in vain of the presence. With undefined feet, barely a sketch of legs, its nature revealed itself elusive. Upon the second questioning, the echo of the figure finally took shape in words. "My name is Ermenegilda de Núñez," she calmly announced, unleashing even more mystery in my grandfather's mind. An unknown yet resonant name, as a shadow from the past mentioned a Colonel Núñez, the previous owner of the house.

- I require your assistance, – uttered the entity with a voice that seemed to emanate from the mist of time. Overwhelmed by disbelief, my grandfather clung to the hammock, asking, – What kind of help do you need? - while Ermenegilda added, – Things that must be done. Following this, she continued, – Come tomorrow at the same time, but come alone, and I will tell you what you must do. As the entity finished the sentence, it faded away in its ethereal form. In his desperation, my grandfather left the room and sought the shelter of his wife, who, with suspicion, weighed whether this commotion was but a ploy to conquer her bedroom.

The next day, the story spread among the household staff as my grandmother shared it with her friends, and as the saying goes, "a small town, a big hell." All day they teased my grandfather about his departure, trying to bridge the gap between him and my grandmother, but the old man ignored the jests. The following night, he decided to return to the spot, but this time accompanied by my mother, who was around four years old at the time. However, this time, there was no presence of the lady.

Had the solitary requirement of her presence not been fulfilled? Did the company of a child drive away the entity? We will never know.

Thus, like the intertwined verses of an endless poem, the stories continue, with enigmas and shadows inscribed in the very essence of the colonial house. My narrative, a humble tribute to the history of the people and families who inhabited the place, continues with the tales of my aunt Lina and the presence of a Romani couple who months later rented what is now my uncle Rene's room. My grandparents decided to lease the place to the Calé[21] couple, who, in a peculiar manner, shared that corner for a brief period before leaving without a trace, without uttering a single explanation.

The fleeting departure of those characters, shrouded in a halo of mystery, never ceased to amaze my

---

[21] Gypsy

grandparents. Their eyes gazed in bewilderment at the space they had occupied, and it was there that their looks encountered an added enigma. In one corner of the room, a rudimentarily made hole, within which rested a "morocota", a silent witness to some hidden secret. Ah, the morocota, that twenty-dollar coin, a jewel of gold and copper in magical proportions: 90 percent golden radiance and 10 percent the warm embrace of copper. On our soil, this precious piece found its home since that distant year, 1830, when banking currents had not yet swayed their waters in our land.

I want to add, for informative purposes, that in the days when souls stored their treasures in clay, those earthen vessels, like buried secrets, awaited in some corner of the home, the "morocota" assumed its role. A refuge for savings, a pillar of certainties in uncertain times, intertwining with history and whispers of the past. I want to make it known that, as the locals say, if a presence from the other world shows you the burial place of gold or some valuable metal, it is advisable to leave part of the burial and not take all its contents. Could this be what Ermenegilda wanted to show my grandfather? Or could this be one of the many burials that over time have appeared in that place? I have the theory that Ermenegilda was not trying to show a gold prize, but rather she needed to expiate some debt or penalty that was not settled in life and that compelled her to return in the presence of the living from time to time. Who knows.

Over the years, the dwelling revealed its supernatural characteristics again as we moved towards the 1960s. A family friend, connected by ties to my parents, crossed the threshold of that house while exploring the paths of Tinaco. During the rest hour, the matriarch of the visiting family reclined in the large hall. A bed, whose memory was vivid in my mind, occupied the right side of the wall adjacent to the entrance. Destinies coincided because in my childhood, more than once, I fell into the slumber of that same bed, although a fearful unease always awakened my being around three in the morning. At those moments, terror, like an unwelcome visitor, clung to me, yet I never dared to confront it with my eyes half-closed.

The woman was unaware of the stories woven in the threads of the past, murmuring around the place. Without realizing it, she lay down, accompanied by her two or three-year-old son. But in the dimness of the early morning, a cold wind of strangeness swept away her tranquility. Something didn't fit. She tried to get up, seeking the comfort of the bathroom, when her gaze encountered something that defied reality: a woman dressed in white, standing at the foot of her bed, fixing her eyes on her.

The woman's intuition didn't need words; in an instant, she understood that the figure had a negative meaning, either for her or her son. The female figure remained in an immobility that transcended hours. Nothing was said between the two presences, only a silent observation from the almost ethereal figure. Eventually, the silhouette faded away, leaving no traces or requests.

The next day, the woman timidly recounted the events of the previous night and asked if it had been a family member who had not presented themselves, but the reaction of those present was clearly an understanding of what had obviously happened. Most likely, Ermenegilda had returned to continue her wandering in sorrow within the walls of that colonial house.

The ancestral corner still held more secrets. Years later, when my existence was added to the world, and I knew these stories and others that time does not allow mentioning here, I had to sleep in the living room of that house, surrounded by cousins and some uncles. Falling asleep was a constant challenge, as the place carried a weight that inspired fear. However, on that night, providence took pity on me and plunged me into the embrace of fatigue, sparing me from witnessing what follows.

While my sister and other cousins lay on the floor, hammocks, and beds, they began joking about the ghosts and apparitions that, as everyone knew, wandered in the house. "Imagine if Ermenegilda appears to us!" one joked. "I would ask her to reveal the place where they hide the 'morocotas'," echoed the collective laughter. "Be careful, she might ask for something in return," warned another. "If it's not too spooky, I wouldn't mind," another responded in a jovial tone.

It's natural for youth to approach life with lightness, and the family atmosphere fostered moments of fun before sleep. Cousins from Caracas and Valencia shared the atmosphere, a purer time when morality held its steadfastness. In those days, family fraternity allowed for genuine interaction.

Laughter and jokes about Ermenegilda and the spirits echoed in the air when suddenly, footsteps were heard in the corridor. These were not ordinary steps but the clinking of military boots, the march of cavalry from days gone by. I want to pause here to describe that Spanish military boots from the 19th century were tall, reaching below the knee. They were made of robust leather, designed for strength and durability. They often had buckles or adjustable straps, creating a characteristic metallic sound when soldiers stood firm before their superiors.

Adding to the mystery, those present claimed to hear the typical sound of a soldier at attention. The sound came right from the threshold of the hall where we were. The shock filled the air, and even the older cousins ran for refuge, towards an aunt's bed. But the sound persisted, defiant, as if it wanted to confront those present. A brother-in-law, assuming the role of a leader, went out to investigate, turned on lights, and scrutinized, but nothing was revealed.

The next day, this narrative became public among all my cousins and uncles, and I thanked the saints because this time I didn't even wake up as usual in the early hours of the morning to feel the weight of the bad vibrations that I normally experienced in that room.

The stories continued their dance, tales of things that hardly find an explanation. But I reserve my final word for one of the most chilling chronicles, the one that intertwines my uncle René with my uncle Pancho, René's brother. This episode occurred in times when they were still walking this world, and for some reason, so close to the departure of both, I feel that the story is somehow linked to that passage.

Not many years ago, it was, when not much time had passed since I headed towards more northern latitudes, leaving my homeland behind. It was then that one day, as shadows lengthened their fingers, Pancho and his driver arrived at the colonial house. Their final destination, Valencia, but time had evaporated, it was too late to hit the road. And as a stroke had subdued my uncle Pancho just a few months ago, traveling long distances was beyond his reach.

It was René, my uncle, who took care of hosting them. He assigned them the old room that had been the dwelling of my grandmother, while he retired to his own chamber. They set out to refresh themselves after the long journey; the driver expressed his need for a glass of water. He left the room, traversing the long corridor toward the kitchen. He passed by the living room, mentioned multiple times, turned left, in front of René's room, and continued, circling the dining room, straight to the kitchen. But upon arrival, he encountered the dimness, and the search for light delayed his encounter with the glasses to fill them with water. And there, while his hands found the rhythm of darkness, his gaze found the corner where a small table rested, carved in stone, and upon it, an elderly woman, lost in thought.

Polite, the driver made an effort in a goodnight greeting, although the lady did not respond. Assuming that perhaps, due to her advanced age, she had not heard, he did not insist. Tired as he was, he sipped the water and returned to the room where my uncle Pancho lay.

It was there, at that moment, when the narration takes on a darker hue. Minutes later, the screams of both men shattered the night, a gut-wrenching startle. To understand the magnitude, it is necessary to first grasp my uncle Pancho. Raised in that dwelling, he had shared his life with these stories, never disturbed by their tales. Now, mature and steadfast in their beings, these men were not prey to trivial impressions. They came from the plains, with strong character, and as is mentioned in the legend of the Silbón[22] when "Juan Ilario[23]" replies to his friend, "I am a man to give a good beating to anyone," these are the men who inhabit these lines.

Soon, René emerged, compelled by what was happening. Although in later accounts from René and my aunt Lina, the precise reason for the terror of those two beings was never clarified. They refused to spend the night in that room for the rest of the night. This is the enigma that has overwhelmed me since then because that entity or whatever it was, manifested a darker aspect.

The next morning, during breakfast and still reliving the previous night in words, the driver asked René to dismiss his sister Lina because he thought the elderly woman, he encountered in the kitchen the night before was the sister mentioned on other occasions. However, my uncle responded with astonishment that Lina had not been in the house; she was in the vicinity of Caracas. Surprise was evident on the driver's face; he urgently wanted to leave that house, as he understood that the phenomena began with his entry into the kitchen.

Months later, my uncle René would have a terrible accident that left him in a lamentable condition, and

---

[22] Famous legend of an evil spirit in Venezuela
[23] Character of Venezuelan literary fantasy

in a profound depression, he made the decision to voluntarily leave his life. Lina found him in his room, leaving behind a letter. I haven't delved into such gloomy details. That man, who once possessed knowledge and elegance, was enveloped by the weight of his acute sensitivity, his greatest weakness. I imagine the pain he inflicted on my aunt Lina, who shared a whole lifetime with her older brother in that dwelling saturated with stories. Lina, in her strength, accepted his choice and faced life head-on.

Time flowed, and as it did, Pancho also departed for better destinations. The house, then, acquired darker and sadder shades. Lina, progressively defeated by the ravages of time, left her home to reside with another sister. The property fell under the control of a former servant, who transformed it into a nest of illicit merchandise and lost all traces of morality. Even Ermenegilda, I imagined, would retreat from the new tenants, hordes that seemed to return from the abyss.

In retrospect, reviewing these tales and others that I keep for other ears, I return to that time machine that, through the anecdotes of our ancestors, allows me to glimpse a past populated by characters whose achievements and mistakes go unnoticed by our petty nature.

Based on these stories, I reflect, ghosts may perhaps be conglomerates of feelings, passions, and experiences that remain intertwined with places and people. Perhaps the most bitter or sweet memories, the threads woven in the web of time and space, occasionally manage to interact with us in the plane in which we are given to live. Maybe each person who inhabited that house was the true ghost, entities that passed through this life, loved, hated, suffered, and never understood that they were only specters. It could be that I, as the narrator of this story, am also a ghost because we do not understand that we were born dead and that life is only a mirage, a projection of our mistakes and successes, a process that has become infinite through generations of families who insist on believing that things will be different, but the events of life are and will be an endless cycle.

My uncle Antonio

El Baúl, Cojedes state, 1930

"The darker the night, the brighter the stars. The deeper the grief, the closer is God."

- Fyodor Dostoyevsky

My paternal grandparents, amidst the whirlwind of life, brought forth a dozen children, of whom only three persevered beyond the ebb and flow of time. Precisely, the last three in an order I allow myself to transcribe: José Antonio, Carmelo Antonio, and Elba. But prior to their arrival, in the loom of my memories, the recollections of two departed uncles, Antonio and Margot, intertwine. Though my personal contact did not extend to them, they seemed to embed themselves in the hearts of my grandparents with threads of profound affection.

Margot, like the legends my grandmother narrated on nostalgic afternoons and corroborated by the testimonies of my uncles, was a creature of sublime beauty who graced this world for only the brief span of a year. With golden hair and blue eyes, gifts inherited from my grandfather, it is easy to envision her as the treasure of the old man's weary eyes. However, the unfortunate airs of that time, when penicillin had not yet cast its light, and medical knowledge was rudimentary, prevented Margot from unfolding the fullness of her beauty to the world—the charm that only time and experience transform into radiant maturity.

I always picture her through the stanzas of an old song, masterfully interpreted by the voice of Leo Marini[24], whose title coincides with my aunt's name and goes like this:

"And she said goodbye,

her name was Margot,

she wore a blue beret

and on her chest hung a cross."

"Farewell, Margot!" my grandparents would exclaim there, in the serene cemetery, as your soul soared towards the realms of ethereal dreams. You depart, and I remain in these forgotten lands of God.

I envision how they would clothe her in a little white dress, crafted from exquisitely woven cotton. Her summer shoes, light as her dreams, surely rested on her porcelain feet. And on her head, a white bow radiating purity, accentuating the delicacy of her snowy little head. This image resonates in my mind, an evocation that becomes an ancestral thread connecting my present to the echoes of the past.

---

[24] Argentine singer and actor from the 1940s of the 20th century.

This tale also stirs the memories of my father, recounting family stories to his friends, strands of memory that weave the figure of Margot and sing the same song that, like an ancient echo, lingers in the melody of my thoughts. Now, I am the witness uttering "farewell, Margot," carrying in my voice the echo of farewell to the young aunt who departed too soon. Farewell, Margot! You join the circle that embraces my grandparents and my father, in an embrace of times converging in the beyond.

But the pain did not find its end with Margot, as it is told that within a single year, they lost up to two children. Simple colds and bacterial infections claimed the most vulnerable, and the definitive blow came with the farewell of Antonio. Antonio, the pride of Don Chucho, his favorite son and heir by antonomasia. My father's memories paint a picture of an intelligent young man, radiant with joy, bold and handsome. He possessed everything one could desire, and as an additional fruit, he stood out for his dedication to his studies. He was destined to take the family business to unexplored heights, paving the way for our family to ascend to the highest rungs of the nation. However, everything faded away before the relentless onslaught of a fever that in present days would be resolved in a brief span of two or three days of recovery.

Just as in the tale of one who walked among the poor and the dispossessed, misfortune began on a

Wednesday tinted with rain, an Ash Wednesday, emblematic evocation of the ephemeral nature of human life, a reminder of both our fragility and the need to amend, to prepare the soul for the arrival of Easter. On this day, Antonio's journey towards the embrace of death commenced. The young man set out in the company of friends to enjoy rural activities, explore the waters of the river, visit companions, and perhaps, steal the heart of some girl. Yes, a rainy day and an evening cold marked the beginning of his misfortune.

"Offer lemon juice, Mrs. Margarita; lemon is effective against the flu," the maid would suggest to my grandmother. Although the lemon failed to alleviate the illness, and the fever loomed over Antonio during Thursday afternoon.

Aware of the gravity of the situation and mindful of the previous losses of his other children, Don Chucho dispatched a doctor to the state capital. The cost did not matter; he was willing to invest his entire fortune to save Antonio. However, in those times, the journey from San Carlos to El Baúl was challenging, and money, unlike faith, could not move mountains.

The night progressed, and it was already Thursday when the song of a screech owl echoed on the roof of the house. This bird had a peculiar, mournful cry, somber like a human lament. In the Venezuelan plains, belief held that if the screech owl sang in a house where there was a sick person, it was a sign that the person was destined to depart. Beside himself, the old man seized his rifle and rushed outside, firing frenziedly at the ominous bird.

-   Go away, devil's bird, cease your hellish sound. You won't take my son! - the man shouted, as his shots missed in the darkness. Anger and fear overwhelmed him, forcing him to reluctantly return inside against his will.

Friday arrived, and with it, the final farewell. The fever took him swiftly, expiring at the ninth hour as if trying to emulate Jesus on the cross. The mother wept inconsolably, while the father lost his sanity. Relatives hurried to organize the wake, as Chucho had lost all lucidity. The fear of possible contagion hastened the preparations.

On Saturday, the grief persisted. Chucho noticed that his son's dog was not roaming nearby, and, following an intuition, he headed to the cemetery. There, the dog was, paws bloodied from the tireless effort to dig into the earth, fervently seeking to free his beloved owner. The dog's lament echoed like the cry of an infant, and at that moment, the old man collapsed beside the grave, mourning the loss of his boy. There was no Easter Saturday nor Resurrection Sunday; no angel appeared to say, "Why seek ye the living among the dead?" The good news never arrived.

Three days and three nights, the old man clung to his son's grave. Finally, they found him and forcibly brought him back home. But for the canine, the story was even more tragic. No matter how much they kept him away from the burial site, the dog returned again and again, until they eventually found him lifeless beside his already deceased master. The dog resisted until his last breath, remaining loyal to the end.

I can conclude that the true ghost in this story was the figure of my grandfather, who thereafter navigated life without a clear direction. He seemed to have become a wandering soul, where resentment and bitterness overflowed towards everything and everyone. His businesses faded away, and the once prosperous and prominent family in the region fell into oblivion, buried like the rest of my uncles.

The Black Hammock

Arismendi, Barinas State 1936

"The crimes carry their punishment on their backs."

- Miguel de Cervantes

This narrative is set in the gloomy period when my paternal grandfather was thrust into the clutches of the Great Depression of the thirties, an economic crisis that ravaged the globe and, in the case of Venezuela, left a trail of ruined merchants, including my grandfather's endeavors. Transitioning from a man of prosperity, he found himself immersed in financial troubles, forced to liquidate what little remained and abandon the town of El Baúl, seeking refuge in the locality of Arismendi.

The municipality of Arismendi is one of the twelve that make up the state of Barinas in Venezuela. Nowadays, it houses around 21,000 inhabitants, but back then, the population was minimal. The distance separating Cojedes from Arismendi, in Barinas, stretches about 133 kilometers, firmly placing us in the vastness of the plains. Anecdotes my father used to share hinted that this region was more rugged, where the labor of laborers started at four in the morning, sustained only by a steaming cup of coffee. My grandfather's decision to venture into the plains might be influenced by the fact that my grandmother hailed from those parts; he likely had the support of relatives in the area.

However, my aim is not to delve into the details of my family's migration between these territories but rather into the anecdote my father claimed had its roots in those lands. Personally, I haven't found conclusive evidence that this story is exclusively Venezuelan; it might be a compilation of legends that took shape in different corners of Spanish America, adapting according to the location where it was told.

In this continuation, I am pleased to share the tales as I heard them from my father's words. During that time, a man emerged, whom we shall call Julian Salcedo since his precise name escapes my memory. This individual frequented the bed of a married woman, unbeknownst to her husband. Every Saturday, he mounted his horse and headed to the wattle and daub shack where this lady resided, aware that her husband would be absent, as he ventured into hunting every weekend and returned on Sundays.

As often happens in these situations, the tension escalated, giving rise to hatred and gossip that flooded the town. Julian's mother, a woman of faith and good character, notably affected by her son's behavior, strongly reproached him for his actions and implored him to abandon that path, as it tarnished the honor of the family and his own.

Julian, stubborn and proud, responded insolently to his mother. However, the lady, overflowing with kindness and integrity, had no choice but to forgive him and entrust his protection to the spirits, fervently wishing for him to change his course. Despite this, Julian mounted his horse and headed towards his clandestine affair.

The shack was a two-hour ride away, but barely 30 minutes into his journey, he spotted in the distance a procession accompanying a black hammock. Approaching, he inquired in a plainsman's tone:

- Where you off to, mate?

A man with a wide-brimmed hat responded, his face concealed beneath the shadow, making it difficult to discern his features:

- We're takin' this passed soul to his restin' place.

Driven by the curiosity that already consumed him, Julian continued with the following question:

- An' who's the feller we're takin' to his restin' place?

- His name is Julian Salcedo – the interlocutor under the hat replied.

Julian experienced a shiver that ran through his body. Although he tried to scrutinize the face of the figure in the hammock, it remained hidden and enigmatic. Nevertheless, he continued his journey. Not even twenty minutes passed when he encountered another similar procession, carrying yet another black hammock. He quickened his pace, and upon facing the group, repeated his question to learn the identity of the deceased. The response he received left him dumbfounded: his own name echoed in his ears once more. Leaning towards considering a strange coincidence, he took hold of his beast's reins and continued on his way. Nothing and no one could prevent him from reaching his desired destination.

As he approached the ranch where the woman awaited him, a hill covered the vast savannah where the modest dwelling was situated. Once again, a similar procession crossed his path, composed of mourning men carrying a black hammock. Julian, once more, cast his question into the air:

- Where are you headed?

He received the same response that the previous processions had provided. With the departure of the procession, a deep fear seized Julian; his blood ran cold, and his legs weakened, succumbing to the typical stomach discomfort of fear. On the brink of crossing the hill and venturing into the plain that revealed his long-awaited destination, he made a radical decision: he turned his mount and headed back to the town of Arismendi.

What Julian was unaware of was that the woman's husband had discovered his infidelities and had coerced his wife into inviting the wrongdoer. The husband lay in wait in the right place to, at the opportune moment, eliminate the thief of his affections.

Were the spirits the ones who repeatedly warned him of imminent danger? Did his mother's prayers activate the intervention of angels to protect him? Was it simply a triple coincidence? I leave it to the reader to choose the interpretation they find most fitting.

Creole Balls

Cojedes State, inland plains, 1938

"The disordered soul carries in its guilt the pain."

- San Agustín

This tale originates directly from my father, who swore until his last days that it was entirely true. The events I am about to narrate unfolded exactly as I will relate them.

I wish to commence this narrative by emphasizing a unique quality of my father: his skill in storytelling. Whether recounting legends of the plains or his own experiences, he possessed the gift of infusing them with an unparalleled allure, making listening to him a genuine pleasure. His descriptions were like strokes of a brush vividly painting characters and landscapes, bringing them to life as if you were watching a film on the big screen. His imitations of sounds and gestures of the narrated characters immersed you entirely in the story.

Of course, to be fair, I must stress that this ability is typical of those hailing from the Venezuelan plains, where oral narration is a fundamental way of transmitting knowledge and experiences, especially in such a challenging environment. In the past, when technology was scarce, these skills were essential for survival in those lands. Unfortunately, today, the young plainsmen have largely forsaken these marvelous traditions in favor of their mobile devices and pre-defined messages, often contributing nothing positive. I also want to mention that it was evident to me the effect sharing a story involving my grandfather had on my father. His face would light up with a distant joy, yet simultaneously convey a profound respect for the memory of his progenitor.

Thus, having established this context, I proceed to share the story at hand. Some time ago, in rural Venezuela, where most people traveled on horseback or mule, my grandfather decided to take my father, who was then only about eight years old, on one of his journeys from the town of El Baúl to the western plains. For my father, this opportunity to travel with my grandfather and the laborers who were part of his entourage was like embarking on an invaluable adventure, akin to visiting "The Treasure Island" from Robert Louis Stevenson's novel. Riding across the vast plains, sailing in a bongo to the lands of Apure[25], and perhaps reaching Capanaparo[26], passing through San Fernando[27] and venturing further south into the lands of Cinaruco[28]. Even in the present day, this would be a lengthy

---

[25] Venezuelan state
[26] The Capanaparo River has its source in Colombia. Passing into Venezuela, Apure State, before joining the Orinoco.
[27] San Fernando de Apure is a city in Venezuela, capital of the state of Apure.
[28] It is a river on the border in Venezuela and Colombia.

journey, and in those times, with scarce modern transportation, it must have been quite an odyssey.

I imagine my grandfather addressing my father with these words: "Look, Carmelito, get ready, because tomorrow I leave on a business trip, and I'll take you with me so you can learn." It must have been a great privilege that the old man chose him over his older brother, José Antonio.

My father recounts that the journey unfolded without any issues, and the vastness of the plains left a profound impression on him. The herons, the caimans, the "madrinas de orejanos[29]," and an endless horizon that stretched like an ocean across a plain that seemed to have no end. They advanced throughout the day until the calm evening fell, the sun dipped into the horizon, staining it with an intense red before disappearing entirely. It was at that moment when they spotted a hamlet in the distance. My grandfather decided it was prudent to spend the night there, as there was no other nearby place for shelter.

Once they arrived at the location, they were greeted by an old overseer from a nearby cattle ranch. This man wore tattered pants and a worn-out shirt. After the customary greeting in that region, my grandfather inquired if it would be possible for him, his son, and the laborers accompanying him to

---

[29] wild cattle

spend the night in a place that provided shelter. The farmer, in a friendly manner, pointed out that they could stay in the small house at the back since it was no longer in use. The dwelling was partially in ruins, but it retained the typical architecture of Venezuelan houses from that era, with a porch surrounding the house and an internal courtyard providing relief from the heat of the plains.

After securing the mules in the corral and hanging hammocks along the porch, my grandfather and father shared a hammock in the center, with a laborer on each side. My grandfather instructed the trusted laborer to have the Mauser[30] ready just in case, although he himself carried a .38 caliber revolver prepared at his waist.

The night arrived swiftly, bringing with it the deafening chorus of millions of crickets that seemed to form an orchestra of vibrant sounds, along with other nocturnal noises. It didn't take long for them to fall asleep, but being true plainsmen, they knew it wasn't advisable to completely surrender to fatigue. My grandfather and the laborers kept one eye half-open, alert to any possible mishaps.

It was then, around one in the morning, when a sound of "thuds" on the ground, like the rolling of a ball beneath the hammocks, traversed the hallway and culminated in a dull "thud" against one of the

---

[30] German rifle

walls at the end of the porch. The sound persisted: "run, run, run," until it finally collided with the wall with a "thud" that startled everyone present. My grandfather took out a flashlight to try to uncover the cause of this strange phenomenon, but they couldn't discern any details that would indicate its origin.

After a few frustrating minutes of being unable to grasp the reason behind these noises, they prepared once again to go to bed when, once more, the object rolled down the hallway and struck the wall.

- Blimey! Is it some sort of critter, then? Or maybe them folks from the neighboring house are having a laugh with us? - my grandfather wondered aloud. However, before he could finish expressing his suspicions, the object rolled again beneath their hammocks: run, run, run, thud.

My grandfather decided to use his flashlight to illuminate the object just as it passed under his hammock, hoping to uncover its nature. But the moment the light reached it, the noise abruptly ceased. It seemed as if the mysterious entity understood it was being observed and concealed its true nature. My grandfather tried several times to catch it off guard, but every time he illuminated it, the sound immediately stopped.

Run, run, run, silence. That's how it worked each time the flashlight was turned on.

It was then that the trusted laborer, in his typical llanero[31] accent, suggested - Blimey, that looks to be a restless spirit, it does. We'd best say a Our Father and a Rosary, we would.

So, they began reciting prayers, and for a few minutes, the entity heightened its presence. Its movements became more continuous, and the sounds more defined. My father, clinging fearfully to my grandfather's body, didn't fully understand what was happening but joined in the process of prayer. Finally, after reciting the last prayer of the Our Father, the noise ceased without any explanation.

I imagine it was extremely difficult for my father to fall asleep that night. Surely, he constantly checked for my grandfather's presence and ensured his predecessor remained vigilant in case that entity returned "to take him by the legs," as the older folks used to say in those times regarding spirits that took away mischievous children, although this didn't seem to be the reason for this situation. In the end, sleep must have prevailed, and the day dawned without incidents, accompanied by the singing of birds and the refreshing morning breeze.

Before departing, they were invited to have breakfast with the locals, and during the meal, my grandfather raised the issue of the nocturnal

---

[31] Venezuelan Cowboy

incident they had witnessed. Before he could finish his question, he noticed an expression on the faces of the villagers that revealed both acceptance and knowledge of the situation. An elderly man present approached and offered an explanation that left everyone bewildered:

- Look, sir, what ye heard yesterday ain't the first time it's been told to us. Every soul spendin' a night in that corridor mentions the noise of somethin' rollin' from one side to t'other, clatterin' against the wall. It kicks off near the 'nails' and keeps at it for a spell, or 'til folks decide to make a quick exit 'cause of whatever might be stirrin' up that ruckus.

Our interlocutor continued with his rural accent the account, – A yesteryear tale unfolds in that nook, where a proper shindig kicked off years ago. The folks drowned themselves in spirits, and betwixt the revelry and the high spirits, they lost their senses and brewed up a hullabaloo that not even the rosary could reckon with. Back in them times, a stern "gomero[32]" civil head honcho ruled these parts. Ignorin' such capers wasn't his way, so he dove into restoring order to that raucous, that Gomorrah they had goin' on. Blimey! What the man didn't know was that these folks were downright nasty, and upon entering the house, they cleaved his head off with a machete. But the tale doesn't end there, 'cause after they splattered his brains, they started playing bowls

---

[32] Regarding the Venezuelan dictator Juan Vicente Gomez

with his noggin thudding against the wall. Since then, the poor bloke's spirit haunts the place, seemingly seeking to ease its guilt so it can finally rest in peace.

The impact on the guests was profound, and my grandfather decided to light a candle and pray again before leaving, hoping to contribute to the release of the lingering soul. After the farewell, they mounted their horses and slowly rode away. The hamlet gradually vanished from their sight, much like the sorrows of the village chief and the sins of the locals, as the horizon stretched out before them.

The scream of death

Valencia, Carabobo state, 1996

"Fear is my most faithful companion; it has never deceived me to go with another."

- Woody Allen

I can attest to the veracity of this anecdote, as I was its protagonist. Though it may seem fantastical and spine-chilling, the events I am about to recount occurred just as I narrate them. These incidents transpired during my engineering studies in the city of Valencia, while I resided in a student dormitory located directly across from the polytechnic institute. This abode was exceptionally convenient, as I only had to cross the street to reach the educational institution, saving me money on transportation and time, an invaluable resource in a city like Valencia.

The dwelling in question was a two-story structure with an exterior garden surrounded by a concrete wall. Access to the place could be gained through two means: a rear door leading to an inner courtyard, typically used for tending to animals—I should note that the owner was a veterinarian by profession. The other option was the front main door, after passing through a gate between the outer walls. The interior of the house exuded a palpable melancholy. Its furniture was worn and dilapidated;

luxury was alien to its structure. The simple kitchen was on the left upon entry. To the right, after entering, was a small office where the doctor had her tools for attending to arriving pets. Between the office and the other end of the house, a bit more to the left and right in the middle, a staircase rose to the upper floor. Upstairs, a hallway housing two rooms at each end and two more on the sides. The owner occupied the room at the left end, if oriented the same way as upon entering. Both on the ground floor and the upper one, the house displayed signs of decay: peeling paint, walls stained by the passage of time, and an evident overall neglect.

I shared a room in this residence with other fellow students from the same institution, but my good friend Félix Osio also used to visit us daily. It was customary for us to spend time together, enjoying some beers and playing dominoes or engaging in other frivolities. It was not an unpleasant period for me; I learned to develop my social skills, played the guitar, met some women, and was able to relax after a prior period of intense pressure.

Besides Félix, we were accompanied by two brothers from the eastern part of the country, a companion from Barinas, a doctor from Coro who had recently arrived, and another person who, as I understand, hailed from Maracay. Unfortunately, I don't recall the names of any of them, so I will settle for mentioning them based on their places of origin.

One name I can evoke is that of the residence owner, Mirian, and I remember her primarily because months later, she made the decision to voluntarily distance herself from this life for reasons I never fully understood.

It is relevant to highlight that before my experience in Valencia, I spent two years in the state of Amazonas, in southern Venezuela, specifically in Puerto Ayacucho. During that period, I served as an army officer in the Jungle Infantry Brigade of that region. Freshly graduated and being a twenty-one-year-old, officially, I was in charge of communications, though in practice, my task was limited to keeping the soldiers engaged in close-order drills that I deemed obsolete in the face of the military technological advancements of the time. My motivation to continue on that path was scarce, and aside from my responsibilities in the brigade, I used to wander around the city without a defined purpose or spend hours reading in the municipal library.

It was then that the idea occurred to me that it would be a good idea to invest my money in purchasing local handicrafts, hoping that someday they might increase in value beyond those lands. Nowadays, I still ponder upon it, although sadly, I lost all those acquisitions in subsequent years. I remember buying colorful paintings and sculptures, as well as a black sculpture resembling a totem, the size of a three or four-year-old child, carved in a heavy material, possibly a kind of stone (this is to give an idea of its size and weight). In its facial expression, it displayed a mix of birds and other animals that I could never clearly identify, and at the base, a relief depicted feet that could be human, although I cannot assert it with certainty. Picture this totem taking the form of a cylinder, like a small black barrel, and the reliefs presenting an anthropomorphic figure. Many people found it somewhat eerie at first glance, but I appreciated the artistic skill involved in its creation.

Once I concluded my service in those lands, I returned to the capital, and all those handicrafts accompanied me. People at airports and bus stations were curious, as these crafts were not so common outside the Amazonas region. So, they also accompanied me to the city of Valencia during my engineering studies, becoming a notable part of this narrative.

Returning to those times of residence in Valencia, I want to emphasize that what characterized us was our unfriendly behavior towards newcomers. Jokes, some in poor taste, entertained us, and I can say that we all were victims of this modus operandi at least once while living in that place. In this narrative, I want to particularly highlight the person who had recently arrived from Maracay, as he will play a crucial role in this story.

It was just another day in my daily routine. After finishing my evening classes, I headed towards the residence, greeting those present as usual. On this occasion, Mirian had the honor of introducing our newcomer. This individual would join the group of more seasoned tenants, sharing this honor with the doctor. Unlike most, he was not a student; on the contrary, he was already employed. From the beginning, he proved to be a person of good character and affable demeanor, seamlessly fitting into our circle.

That evening, we bought some beers and invited him to join us, as was customary, to play dominoes. Around 9 in the evening, one of the individuals from the east mentioned that paranormal events used to happen in that house, as the tragic death of an elderly woman had occurred there before. We immediately understood that this marked the beginning of one of our typical initiation pranks. Félix began reciting incomprehensible prayers, the companion from Barinas hinted that he was a medium, a concept used by those knowledgeable in the supernatural to refer to individuals who could communicate with beings from beyond. Mirian looked at us with a complicit smile. Each one contributed their touch to the narrative, and after several beers that turned into a bottle of rum, I presented the crucial element: the totem that always accompanied me, as if it were a pet. We went to my room and showed him the structure, insinuating that it had always been present in the house and that it was evidence that the mansion was haunted or, perhaps, cursed. The expression on our new friend's face was one of amazement and bewilderment, either because the stories frightened him or because he wondered what kind of residence he had ended up in, with what kind of people he was sharing.

We kept up the charade until bedtime. Each one retired to their room, and I, with a few too many beers, simply took off my clothes and lay down on the bed, exhausted after a long day. The lights went out, sleep came quickly, and silence filled the house.

Hours later, the effects of the beers and my metabolism woke me with the urgency to urinate. I needed relief, but I found myself in the middle of a dark room that faced a hallway that seemed terrifying. Initially, I moved in bed in an attempt to deceive my body and gain time until the sunlight brought the necessary tranquility to safely go to the bathroom. However, I soon realized that my sphincter would not hold out for so long, and I couldn't afford the embarrassment of wetting the bed. So, with fear in my heart, I decided to get up, open the door of the room, and walk the few steps that separated my room from the bathroom. Brave, right? Fear overcame me as I advanced through the darkness, and the shadows at the hallway door made me fear the worst. I, who was part of the cohort wanting to cast the stone towards the accused, was now judged by divine retribution present every time a joker insists on wasting time on trivial matters.

To reach the bathroom, I would have to pass through the corridor that connected it, and it was even understood by the old tenants that the previous owner of that house had taken his own life by hanging in the frame of one of the doors. It was my belief that upon leaving the room, I would see the specter of the deceased hanging and staring at me menacingly with the intention of judging my misdeeds.

With God's help, I managed to reach the bathroom and close the door to ensure that no "hairy hand[33]," La Llorona[34], "the Silbón[35]", or some wandering devil insisted on sharing the space with me. Allow me to describe the bathroom to you as a small space, with the shower in one corner, a small window on the shower wall, the toilet halfway between the door and the shower, and the sink on one side. The place lacked electrical lighting, so I had to feel my way around until my eyes adjusted to the dimness. That night, the darkness was particularly dense, and the house was on a sparsely traveled street, making the sounds of the night clearly audible. The rhythmic hum of crickets turned into a nocturnal song that filled the air: "crii, crii," "crii, crii." There were also sounds, probably

---

[33] It is a legend of a Venezuelan paranormal entity.
[34] Latin American legend.
[35] It is a legend of a Venezuelan paranormal entity.

from nocturnal birds, something like "pajui," "pajui."

I proceeded to do what I had to do, trying to maintain composure despite the unsettling atmosphere. However, at that moment, a female scream, the most spine-chilling I had ever heard, tore through the night shadows and filled me with indescribable terror. I lost complete control; urine scattered in all directions, even on myself; my muscles clenched, and my voice completely faded. I can attest that those scenes from old movies of the 1930s, where Dracula approaches the protagonist, and she, overcome by terror, cannot utter a word, are absolutely true. What a shame to have to compare myself to those characters from horror films, but I realized that the scriptwriters of that era must have based their work on situations of extreme terror, and I was living a similar experience firsthand.

The scream echoed again, and at that moment, I secured the bathroom door with all my might to prevent anything, whatever it was, from entering to seek me out. I had been part of those who wanted to play a prank on the new tenant, and now I was becoming the victim. I understood in the worst way that one should not play with the unknown. A short time passed without hearing any noise, and when I finally mustered the courage to leave the bathroom, the terrifying howl returned, mimicking the cry of a woman or perhaps a child. I had no choice but to turn to my faith, which I had long forgotten, and began to pray a Our Father.

It's interesting how agnostics and atheists can easily abandon their positions when faced with extreme situations. I, who considered myself a materialist and followed the theories of the modern era, turned to the most incomprehensible abstraction: God. However, the fear was so intense that I couldn't even remember the structure of that beautiful prayer. "Our Father who art in...". No matter how hard I tried, my mind went blank.

In that existential dilemma, the screams of the entity continued incessantly. It was then that I decided to take refuge in the bathtub, as if I were seeking protection in some kind of imaginary cave where the spirits of the night could not reach me. The screams persisted, and I couldn't recall any prayer that could help me. Clearly, this was a punishment for my misbehavior, and possibly only the beginning of something much worse.

I must admit, even at the expense of my pride and dignity, that my eyes were on the verge of shedding tears like a little boy, and my digestive system was on the brink of releasing all the contents consumed the day before. The situation was desperate because if it wasn't a supernatural entity punishing me for my actions, then it would be my roommates who would not stop teasing me the next day for being scared in such a way. I was caught between fear and shame, not knowing which would be worse – a sort of "damned if you do, damned if you don't" scenario.

Then, another scream, but this time I realized it was coming from outside the house. Remembering there was a small window at the top of the bathroom wall, I tried to climb up to see the source of those screams. However, I understood that the window wasn't big enough to stick my head out and look down. Besides, I didn't feel like a hero ready to face whatever it was. I decided to sit down and analyze the situation, searching for an explanation for the screams. There had to be something I was overlooking, something that would make sense of what I was experiencing. I told myself, "You're studying engineering, you understand sciences like mathematics, physics, and chemistry, you've studied psychology, and you understand the relationship between matter and energy." This self-convincing began to gradually clear my mind, and I could filter the sound of the screams to get a better definition of what was happening.

It was then that I realized the scream wasn't produced by a woman or a spirit but by a cat. Later, when I shared this story with a friend from Guárico, he confirmed that the yowls of female cats in heat can be mistaken for the cry of a woman or a child. At that moment, my mind, influenced by the atmosphere I had created and the eerie surroundings of the house, had transformed those sounds into the terrifying wail of La Llorona coming to punish me for my antics. It's interesting to think about how many of the legends we know in Latin America could have a similar origin, based on misunderstandings and misinterpretations that over time have become part of our rich and colorful culture. So, in centuries past, I might have been the inspiration for a new legend—the legend of the scream of death.

The Fireball

South America, 1951

"The insanity in an individual is rare; in groups, parties, nations, and epochs, it is the rule."

- Friedrich Nietzsche

On October 12, 1492, the Great Admiral set foot on the lands of the Indies as he believed and continued to believe until his death. With this event, a challenging relationship would begin, spanning 300 years, where Spanish America would go through various periods, most marked by extreme pain.

It was a birthing process, and it was not an easy birth. From the territories of California to the southernmost tip of Tierra del Fuego, a blending of races, a more or less forced mestizaje, would unfold. Eventually, all these elements converged in a human crucible that would result in the Latin Americans, a hybrid and diverse identity. As the Liberator Simón Bolívar aptly expressed, "We are not Indians or Europeans but rather an intermediate species between the legitimate inhabitants of these lands and the Spanish colonizers."

Beyond debates about the rights of the Spaniards in these lands, it is crucial to highlight that the 300 years of coexistence among these diverse human groups gave rise to a unique cultural wealth. In contrast to other regions of the world where racial segregation prevailed, in Latin America, forced and later voluntary coexistence led to a fusion of traditions, languages, and customs. The result is a varied and multifaceted composition that cannot be easily defined, in contrast to regions in Europe, Asia, Africa, or North America where racial and cultural divisions remained firm due to discriminatory attitudes.

In summary, the history of Latin America is an epic narrative of mestizaje and diversity, forged in the fires of coexistence and conflict, where no race or culture can claim absolute supremacy. It is a testament to the ability of people to adapt, evolve, and flourish amid human complexity.

In the vast loom of history, a surprisingly similar narrative was woven across the expanse of Spanish America. The Spanish soldier arrived, an adventurer, a Catholic of apostolic and Roman persuasion, bearing the vision of a crusader and conqueror. They were not men of timidity or mediocrity on the battlefield. If the wager for my own survival depended on the triumph of an army, I would undoubtedly choose the "Tercios[36]" as my first and most secure option.

Initially, their conquest was stained with blood and desolation, but over time, a sort of negotiated

---

[36] Spanish elite soldier of the 16th century

settlement was more or less established with the remaining indigenous peoples. With the arrival of enslaved hands from Africa, the first cities and haciendas were erected on these lands. Yet, in the vast territories of Peru and Mexico, the gleam of gold and silver added an element that further elevated the magnificence of these places, endowing them with temples and universities that North America dared not even dream of.

It was clear to the Spanish kings that managing all these territories would be very challenging, not only due to their vastness but also because of the unruly nature of the subjects of the Castilian crown in those lands. It was necessary to establish laws to organize the territory, define the rights of the indigenous people, legalize the status of the black population, collect taxes, and instill a sense of civilization. However, it was also necessary to divide their collaborators to avoid granting them too much power. Laws were made, injustices were committed, but somehow the empire survived for 300 years. From the beginning, these lands had a condition that accompanies us to this day, where "laws were obeyed, but not fulfilled," or were fulfilled more or less according to convenience.

When the man in power received a Royal Decree, issued by the monarch based in the capital of the empire, which, if we recall, was initially Toledo, he would read it and realize it was impractical. Then, he would summon politicians and religious figures, reaching an agreement that it would be "obeyed, but not fulfilled." They did not deny the king's authority, but adapted to the reality of the Americas.

It is in this setting that the character who will be the protagonist of this story becomes a part of the narrative. I am referring to Lope de Aguirre, or as he is known in a large part of South America, "The Tyrant Aguirre." He was a nobleman native to Araotz, Oñate, a town in northern Spain, born on November 8, 1510. At the age of 21, he heard of the exploits of the Conquistador Francisco Pizarro[37]. Pizarro had discovered the Inca Empire and, with his Thirteen of Fame and a group of followers numbering no more than 250 soldiers, managed to subdue an empire that stretched from Ecuador, through Peru and Bolivia, to reach Chile and northern Argentina. At the time of its surrender, it had an estimated 12 million souls, making Pizarro's feat arguably surpass the actions of Alexander the Great. It is clear that Pizarro's actions included murder, betrayal, and plunder, but my narrative does not focus on the moral character of the individual but on the events that unfolded.

One particular feat would leave a lasting impact on the psyche of the subjects of the empire. Pizarro forced the Inca Atahualpa to fill a room of several square meters once with gold and twice with silver to secure his release by the Indians loyal to the Inca

---

[37] Conqueror of the Inca empire

emperor. Such a ransom of such value had never been paid before, and the agreement was heinously broken when Pizarro, upon receiving the payment, forced the Inca to take communion and then executed him.

In that turbulent historical backdrop, Lope de Aguirre arrived in the lands of Peru around the year 1536. From the moment of his arrival, his reputation was stained by a dark specter of violence, cruelty, and subversive tendencies. These were times marked by bloody internal conflicts tearing through the heart of Peru, and Aguirre immersed himself in several of these struggles. He was seriously wounded in one, left with a useless leg and his hands marked by the flames of a faulty musket. Perhaps he would have faded into the darkness of oblivion, like many other Spaniards who lived and died in these lands, if not for the capricious twist of fate that intersected him with the Marañones[38] expedition, named after the river, they initially navigated when departing from Peru.

At the helm of this bold expedition was Pedro de Ursúa, leading around 300 Spaniards, nearly a hundred indigenous people, and some black slaves. Aguirre joined this adventure, bringing along his mestiza daughter named Elvira. The objective of the expedition was the quest for the mythical "El

---

[38] The Marañón River is a river that flows entirely in Peruvian territory. At its confluence with the Ucayali River it forms the Amazon River – Wikipedia.

Dorado", the legendary city of the Omaguas, where it was rumored that even the streets were paved with gold. This idea was likely a ruse concocted by the indigenous people who, aware of the Spanish greed for gold, cunningly employed this legend to distract and lead them into the depths of the devouring jungle.

From the outset, the expedition was doomed to failure because its leader, Pedro de Ursúa, was more interested in pleasing his mestiza lover, Inés de Atienza, than in ensuring the order and discipline of such a diverse group. There exists a document titled "Noticias historiales de las conquistas de Tierra Firme en las Indias Occidentales[39]" by Fray Pedro Simon, whose original is housed in the library of the University of California, which I had the opportunity to review. On page 249, it reflects that a close friend of Ursúa warns him of the danger:

"Of all these occasions, one Pedro de Linasco, a resident of Chachapoyas and a great friend of Pedro de Ursua, took the opportunity. He was well-experienced in journeys and had extensive knowledge of many who were on this expedition, as well as the circumstances that often lead to uprisings. He wrote a letter to Ursua, informing him of the suspicions that lingered throughout Peru regarding many of the soldiers he commanded. Due to their criminal and tumultuous nature, they could pose significant problems, and perhaps even be the cause of his death. In particular, he could suspect this of Lorenzo de Salduendo, Lope de Aguirre, Juan Alonso de la

---

[39] Historical news of the conquests of Tierra Firme in the West Indies by Fray Pedro Simon

Bandera, Cristóbal de Chávez, a certain Don Martin, and others he also mentioned. He stated that, despite ten or twelve men more or less, he should not fail to continue his journey and thus pleaded with him to dismiss them from his company.[40]"

Terrible mistake on Ursúa's part not to have taken advice. The saying "A warned war doesn't kill a soldier" holds true, but it seems Ursúa was unfamiliar with it.

In addition to the aforementioned, the relentless jungle also played its sinister role, as disease and hunger joined forces to intensify desperation within the group. The first victim was Ursúa himself, though at that moment, Aguirre chose not to reveal himself as the mastermind, opting instead to use a mere puppet, Fernando de Guzmán, as a temporary facade to lead the senseless odyssey in search of El Dorado in the depths of the Amazon jungle.

It was on the first day of January when Aguirre, along with a dozen followers, caught Ursúa off guard and sewed him up until he was unrecognizable. I can only imagine Ursúa's shock upon seeing the traitors. He would have tried to reach for his sword to confront them because, as I mentioned earlier, the Tercios were not cowards. Moreover, he knew that upon his death, his wife would likely be the next victim and might face violation.

---

[40] Text written in old Spanish

- What's happening? Have you gone mad? – he would say, sword in hand.

- We've come for you, sir, and spare us the nonsense because you know how this is all going to end, – one of his assassins would reply.

The first slash could enter the left side of the abdomen, rendering him incapacitated. Then, all at once, daggers and sabers would add to the assault, primarily targeting the face, blood flowing abundantly, and the groans of a victim who wouldn't die instantly. I have witnessed the bodies of people killed with machetes, and I can testify that the result is truly horrific. Empty eye sockets, partially severed ears, skulls exposing part of the brain's structure for all witnesses to see. This is how the overly confident Ursúa would meet his end, just as those in America met their end when they forgot that these ventures were matters of life or death.

It was Guzmán who appointed his new lieutenants, elevating Aguirre to the position of second in command. Meanwhile, Inés de Atienza found herself compelled to surrender to one of these newly appointed commanders, an individual known as Zalduendo, as the only way to survive amid the growing barbarity surrounding them.

It is told that upon Ursúa's death, Guzmán gathered the army leaders in an assembly to deliberate on future plans. He tried to maintain the idea of discovering and conquering El Dorado because, in a way, this would absolve them of the treasonous process that had taken place. If successful, the king would easily pardon what they had done, as had happened in other successful expeditions.

A justification document was drafted, including a statement and evidence that Ursúa was causing serious harm to the expedition, and all the men in the camp had to sign it. Vandera and Montoya, individuals loyal to Aguirre, approved the measure. Meanwhile, Aguirre remained in the background to better analyze the events.

The document was drafted, and the soldiers were gathered to sign it. Guzmán, as the general, was the first to put his signature on the paper. Next, Aguirre, in his capacity as "maestre"[41] de campo and second in command, signed, but with a unique addition: "Lope de Aguirre, Traitor." The majority were stunned; some felt remorse and understood the mistake they had made, trying to convince Aguirre that this was not the way out.

There is a paragraph in Robert Southey's novel **"The Expedition of Ursúa and the Crimes of Aguirre"** where the author portrays Aguirre as defiant, responding to the pleas of his associates with these words:

---

[41] military position

"Gentlemen, what madness is this? As if what we have done were a mere pastime and not the work of resolute and sensible men! Have we not killed the king's governor, who represented his person and held full powers and authority? And now, are we going to pretend to absolve ourselves of all guilt through writings and processes that we ourselves have concocted, as if the king and his judges would not understand their origin?

We have all participated in the death of the governor, and we have all rejoiced in it; if anyone feels otherwise, let him place his hand on his heart and say so. Thus, we have all been traitors. Let us suppose, then, that we find this land we are seeking, and that we conquer it and settle in it, and that it is ten times richer than Peru, better colonized than New Spain, and that the king would derive greater benefit from it than from all the rest of the Indies combined...

The first bachelor and scribbler who arrives with a commission from His Majesty to investigate our conduct would cut off all our heads; that would be the reward for our services! Therefore, since our lives are already forfeit, my advice is that we sell them dearly, and let us get ahead of those who seek to destroy us by heading to a good land that we all know well and where we have many friends.

When they see the purpose for which we have returned, they will welcome us with open arms, join us, and defend us to the death. That is the path we should take, and for this reason, I have signed as a Traitor."

It should not be surprising that something similar might have been said on the spot, as several later letters Aguirre sent to Emperor Philip II laid out his plan for freedom and self-government in the Americas.

At this point, the expedition was effectively under the ruthless command of Aguirre, who was beginning to lose his sanity. He used any pretext as an excuse to carry out merciless murders. In addition to Aguirre's psychopathy, the humidity, intense heat, and inherent dangers of the jungle contributed to further wear down the expedition.

The savage inhabitants of the jungle, like lurking jaguars, voracious piranhas, formidable six-meter-long caimans, poisonous insects, and hostile indigenous tribes, added an additional element of exhaustion. Those who have experienced the jungle will understand what I mean. Rain is a constant companion, and staying dry is a daunting task. Foot diseases are common among those who wear typical clothing from what they call the "civilized world." Malaria becomes an endemic presence, relentlessly pursuing you. The word "fever" becomes part of the daily vocabulary, as it is a fever that never seems to leave you, though for some Europeans who lack the necessary defenses, it proves to be deadly, not allowing them time even to savor it.

Aguirre devised a strategy of attrition based on sabotage and intrigue because his goal was no longer El Dorado, nor had it ever been. His mission was rebellion against everything and everyone. Years of resentment and deprivation had accelerated his taste for absolute destruction, including his own. He was willing to defy the king and even God if necessary. First, he sank several barges to introduce a delay in the mission, then came the selective murders. Valcazar was one of the first, followed by Vandera and Cristóbal Hernandez. Executions increased in number, some without any basis, and thus, the already limited power of Guzmán, the supposed new leader of the expedition, diminished. Speaking of Guzmán, it is known that they had reached the absurd imposition of a supposed coronation as the prince of Peru. Since the new leader was an easily manipulated man, he accepted such nonsense, giving Lope de Aguirre time to dismantle what was left of the expedition.

The same fate befell Zalduendo, the new lover of Ursúa's late wife, so that later, Aguirre's henchmen stabbed Doña Inés to death, and she was quite possibly also violated in the process. The bloodshed here seemed endless. The priest Henao, Serrano, and Baltazar, as well as Guzmán himself, who died from a musket shot in one of the typical treacherous maneuvers of the murderer Aguirre.

With Guzmán dead, Lope de Aguirre took complete control of the remaining men. The Spaniards, either out of fear of the new leader or because they were so entrenched in his madness, followed him without hesitation. The indigenous people who had been part of the entourage from the beginning had abandoned the expedition, escaping into the jungle, leaving behind some black slaves. Alongside Aguirre, his mestiza daughter continued, and according to rumors, their relationship did not represent a proper interaction between father and daughter.

On March 23, 1561, Aguirre urged 186 captains and soldiers to sign a declaration of war against the Spanish Empire, proclaiming himself Prince of Peru, Tierra Firme, and Chile. The impact of this action was so profound that centuries later, the liberator Simón Bolívar wrote that Lope de Aguirre's rebellion was the first declaration of independence of a region in America. However, I see in the Tyrant Aguirre that terrible germ typical of the Hispanic world, where military disobedience opposes institutions symbolizing law and order. The king, even if an absolute monarch, symbolized institutions, and the security of laws, even if those laws were not always equally enforced. But Aguirre was anarchy, where there is surely no option to be respected or upheld by justice in any way.

The route that Lope de Aguirre took from that point has not been clear to historians, but based on, my knowledge of that region, it is plausible that he entered the "Rio Negro" a big river from the upper part of the Amazon River. Following the course of the Rio Negro, he would have reached the other great river of South America, the Orinoco River. Following a course around the dense jungle, he could have advanced towards the central territory, passing along the sides of the central and eastern plains of Venezuela, with the goal of finally reaching the mouth of the Atlantic.

What might have been Aguirre's and the other insubordinate's thoughts at this stage of the journey? Aguirre had become the leader of a fictitious nation, a nation of thieves, murderers, and resentful individuals seeking revenge for the hardships fate had bestowed upon them in those distant lands of the Indies. There was no gold or silver for this mission; there were only endless jungles, infinite savannas, mountains touching the sky, and that was the wealth that emperors and Spanish conquerors never understood in the Americas. The nation of the Marañones, as Aguirre liked to call his followers, was one of the first expeditions of Europeans to venture into the Orinoco River and the heart of a jungle that does not befriend men who are foreign to it. The sight of the confluence of the black-colored Caroní River and the mighty brown-colored Orinoco River, their waters not mixing for several kilometers due to the force of their currents, must have been an astonishing and mysterious spectacle for these adventurers. Or seeing the width that the Orinoco achieves in the region of the Delta Amacuro, where it can reach a thickness of twenty-two kilometers during the rainy season. These poor souls who had crossed the "Ocean Sea"[42] and now found themselves in such a different world, with beauty incomparable as it was malevolent, so distant from the balanced European nature because in the jungle, nothing is constant, nothing is homogeneous. Flooded lands, giant trees that block the sunlight, and where the earth lives in eternal night, animals that seemed drawn from the tales of "One Thousand and One Nights"[43], humans who blended with the surrounding nature. Death is a fundamental part of the jungle because from the falling leaves that nourish these mineral-resource-poor lands to the decomposition of millions of insects and animals of all kinds, they sustain the cycle of life and death that is so common in those lands.

It is in Aguirre's letter, written months later and addressed to Emperor Philip II, where we can infer the true emotional and psychological state of our character. This document, written in "Nueva Valencia"[44] and delivered to a friar, is a fundamental testimony to understanding the early years of the conquest of America and reveals a man who was not lacking in education but also carried the burden of accumulated resentment over the years and an explosive and sometimes incoherent personality. These excerpts from his letter offer a

---

[42] Ocean Sea was the name given to the Atlantic Ocean in Spain at that time.
[43] The Arabian Nights is a medieval compilation of traditional oriental tales.
[44] Venezuelan city.

glimpse into the turbulent and dark world in which Lope de Aguirre and his group of followers found themselves amid the relentless and enigmatic jungle:

"In my youth, I traversed the Ocean Sea to the lands of Piru[45], deeming it worthy to wield the lance and fulfill the duty owed by every honorable man. Thus, for twenty and four years, I have rendered many a service in Piru, engaging in the conquest of natives and the establishment of settlements in your service. Particularly, I have partaken in battles and encounters waged in your name, ever in accordance with my strength and capability, without burdening your officials for pay or succor, as attested by your Royal records. I truly believe, most excellent King and lord, that for me and my companions, you have not been just, but rather cruel and ungrateful for the sterling services we have provided. Although I also believe that those who scribe to you from these distant lands may deceive you.

I forewarn you, Spanish King, in a realm where justice and rectitude abound, befitting the noble vassals you possess in these lands. Regrettably, I, unable to endure further the cruelties perpetrated by your Auditors, Viceroy, and Governors, have renounced your obedience, along with my companions whose names I shall presently disclose. Thus, estranged from our homeland, Spain, we have embarked upon waging upon you in these parts the most ruthless war that our strength may sustain and supply. King and lord, believe this to be a consequence of our inability to endure the great

---

[45] This was the name of the country of Peru at that time.

injustices, exactions, and unjust punishments meted out by your ministers, offspring, and servants. Our fame, life, and honor have been usurped, and it pains the heart to hear the ill-treatment we have suffered."

Proceeds in another paragraph with his complaints and sets forth:

"Behold, behold, Spanish King, that thou be not cruel unto thy vassals nor ungrateful, for while thy father and thou didst reign in the realms of Castile without any distress, thy vassals, at the cost of their blood and wealth, have bestowed upon thee as many realms and dominions as thou dost hold in these parts. Consider, O King and lord, thou canst not, with the title of just King, claim any interest in these lands where thou didst venture naught, without first compensating those who have toiled and labored in this land."

Then he confesses to his cruel deeds in subsequent paragraphs:

"This wicked Governor was so perverse, ambitious, and wretched that we could no longer endure him. Therefore, as it is impossible to recount his villainies and to consider myself a party in my case as they deemed, I shall speak no more, excellent King and lord, save that we did slay him, indeed, a swift death. Subsequently, we raised up a young knight from Seville, who went by the name of Don Fernando de Guzman, as our King, swearing allegiance to him, as your Royal person shall witness through the signatures of all those present. He now resides on the isle of Margarita in these Indies. They appointed me as his Field Marshal, and because I would not tolerate his insults and wickedness, they sought to slay me. I, in turn, slew the new King, the Captain of his Guard, the Lieutenant General, four captains, his Steward, his Chaplain, a cleric of the Mass, a woman in league against me, a commander from Rhodes, an admiral, two ensigns, and another five or six of their allies.

With the intent of continuing the war or perishing in it, due to the numerous cruelties your ministers inflict upon us, I appointed new captains and a sergeant-major. They sought to kill me, and I hanged them all as our march continued, enduring all these deaths and ill fortunes."

We can continue the tale of our story when Aguirre, having reached the Atlantic through the mouth of the Orinoco, set course for "Margarita Island"[46], where his deeds would be etched into the memory of its inhabitants to this day. There is a village with his nickname, "El Tirano," originally known as the port of Paraguachi. Although it was renamed Port Fermín during the independence era, it has maintained the name of our character to this day, as locals and outsiders still refer to it in the same way. This adventurer, who traveled from Peru through the Marañón or Amazon River, arrived one Monday afternoon on June 20, 1561, at the tranquil shores of Margarita Island. They came in two brigantines, one commanded by Martín Pérez and the other by Lope de Aguirre, both of which docked on the beaches of

---

[46] Venezuelan Caribbean island.

Paraguachí to initiate the horrifying massacre of the island's inhabitants.

Unaware of the dark history of this unfortunate expedition, the islanders trusted the requests of the band of outlaws. Aguirre used his wiles to make them welcome the newcomers, providing them with food and supplies, unsuspecting of the impending atrocity. He used a few displays of gold to make them believe that they came willing to share wealth for supplies. Once settled on the island, the intruders perpetrated an unprecedented act of violence: they murdered the Governor and all influential figures in the community. Not content with this, they set houses, farms, and churches ablaze, leaving a trail of destruction and chaos. Robbery, rape, and murder became their distinctive traits.

It is said that they took turns violating the same woman, and age was no limitation for them. A child of a few years was as good a target as an elderly person in their final days.

Among the victims was an ancestor of Simón Bolívar, Ana de Rojas. Tragically, Ana lost her life along with more than 50 people, including men, women, and children, in an act devoid of any mercy. This band of thugs demonstrated a ruthless cruelty that left an indelible scar on the island's history and in the memory of its inhabitants. Ana de Rojas's tragic fate was sealed due to an act of supposed hospitality. She had been forced to shelter one of the Marañon deserters, a man named Alonso de Villena, in her home. However, in a regime where there were no rules or laws other than the impulsive whims of Lope de Aguirre, this action cost her life. She was condemned to be hanged for harboring a deserter, even before Villena declared himself as such. The punishment was particularly brutal, as while they hanged her, she was used as target practice for the hordes of bandits surrounding her. Ana de Rojas's husband did not escape the violence of this ruthless group either. He was murdered on his own estate, in an act of barbarism, alongside a Dominican priest who unfortunately happened to be in the wrong place at the wrong time. These accounts reflect the extreme cruelty and lack of mercy that characterized Aguirre and his followers in the midst of their madness and unrestrained violence.

It is written in the chronicles of Robert Southey that, in his absolute madness, Aguirre ordered the governor and his people to be transferred to a room, likely in the castle of Pampatar. The author mentions that Aguirre relished playing with the psyche of the poor souls, indicating to them that it was merely a transfer to ensure their own safety. One can imagine that Aguirre's visage betrayed his true intentions, and the condemned knew in advance their grim fate. They were all executed; in some works, like Otero Silva's, it is stated that skulls were shattered, introducing a kind of morbid pleasure for El Tirano. This suggests that we are dealing with a psychopathic personality who took pleasure in killing.

However, it is also evident that this character, Lope de Aguirre, carried out these atrocities with the intention of committing his followers in such a way that they couldn't retreat or betray him by joining the opposing side. He was fully aware that his actions were so infamous that there would be no possibility of forgiveness from the authorities. By pushing his followers into such deplorable acts, Aguirre sought to maintain absolute control over them, ensuring they had no escape and remained loyal, even if it was out of fear of the terrible consequences of betraying him. His strategy was to build an unbreakable bond of loyalty based on fear, sin, and desperation.

The death of his field master, named Pérez, adds another grim episode to the escalation of violence and chaos that characterized Lope de Aguirre's regime during his stay on the island. The reasons behind his death may have ranged from a real betrayal attempt to Aguirre's simple paranoia. However, what this made clear was that no one was safe under the rule of such an unbalanced and dangerous individual as Aguirre.

Over time, other collaborators also fell out of favor, and if they were not executed by hanging, they fell victim to the garrote or knife, further accentuating the atmosphere of terror prevailing among Aguirre's followers. His leadership was marked by ruthless cruelty and paranoia that led to a series of bloody purges within his own group, where distrust and fear reigned supreme. After nearly wiping out all the inhabitants of the island, as the only survivors were those who managed to hide in the mountains, the tyrant headed towards the mainland's coast, specifically reaching the shores of Borburata.

This was a settlement with a few houses, a church – which I believe still stands today – all clustered around a walled square that served as protection against constant pirate attacks. It is thought that Aguirre arrived with four vessels, 150 men, two horses, 30 mounts, six artillery pieces, and 100 muskets, giving him a notably strong force for the sparsely defended Venezuelan territory. It should be noted that Venezuela never represented a significant territory for the Spanish crown and was one of the poorest and most forgotten regions of the peninsular government, meaning its defense fell on the locals, and their resources were very limited. Coupled with the fact that these bandits were seasoned in the civil wars of Peru and accustomed to gunfire exchanges, it put serious pressure on the people inhabiting this region.

The tragedy of Aguirre was that he failed to comprehend that this was the true path to attempt success in his disjointed project, as his original plan to continue to Peru was doomed to fail. He could never have the necessary tools to face the regular army of the Spanish crown. If he had strengthened his position in the Venezuelan plains and garnered the support of indigenous people and enslaved Africans, who knows how events might have unfolded.

The situation in Borburata was tense, and the locals were already aware of the numerous violent acts that had occurred on Margarita Island, where even the governor himself had been executed. Amidst their fear, they watched from the hills as Lope de Aguirre and his men disembarked.

The invaders might have marked their presence by driving a sword into the sand, a symbolic gesture of territorial claim for those times. Aware of the villagers' unease, Aguirre sent a group of soldiers to the town to convey a message of reassurance. They assured them that they had no reason to fear, as there were no resources or wealth for them to exploit.

In the midst of this situation, the soldiers encountered one of the deserters who had escaped from Margarita. Once captured, this man managed to save his life by arguing that he had been deceived by the others and, being loyal, had decided to rejoin Aguirre's noble cause. We will never know if Aguirre fully believed his story, but he couldn't afford to lose more men at that moment, so he decided to reintegrate him into his ranks.

This story illustrates the complexity and uncertainty of the events at that time, where loyalty and alliances could be volatile, and decisions were made in extremely difficult circumstances.

However, there were other desertions, and when they tried to offer similar excuses, Aguirre ordered them to be hanged without hesitation. In the book titled "Lope de Aguirre, predecessor of American independence," the author somewhat playfully recounts that one deserter wanted to see with his own eyes whether they had reached the mainland or an island, and that's why he had distanced himself from the group. Aguirre ordered him to be hanged from the tallest tree to dispel his uncertainty. This unhealthy sense of black humor among our conquistadors has persisted to this day, passing through figures like Boves[47], the royalist general in the Venezuelan War of Independence, and also in the Federal War, where General Zamora would arrive in a town and order the execution of everyone present. If a subordinate reminded him that there were children among them, he would respond with sarcasm, urging him to quickly carry out the orders, as there was no need to leave enemies for the future. This dark humor was also present in the dictator Juan Vicente Gomez when he closed universities

---

[47] Spanish soldier

due to protests, saying with a certain wit, "I am treating them like a strict father. Didn't they want to study? I teach them to work." Our leaders have used these ways, unfortunately trivializing the tragedy of our people.

After this incident, Aguirre ordered his men to incinerate the four ships that had transported them from Margarita, as well as everything that remained anchored in the port. With this gesture, he made it clear that there was no turning back; the only path he saw was the confrontation against his Majesty, the King. Henceforth, his temperament became completely unstable. Often, he spared the lives of the sick only to later subject them to execution, accompanied by messages filled with mockery and disdain.

Nights were reddened by the glow of his drunken revelries, and desertions continued like a constant shadow. One of the deserters, known as Alarcón, was recovered by the mayor of Borburata. In a dark pact, with Aguirre holding his daughter and wife hostage, the surrender of Alarcón was negotiated. Without hesitation, the Tyrant agreed to return the women but only to satisfy his perverse pleasure in capturing the traitor. His bloodlust drove him to dictate Alarcón's public execution, dragging him through the streets and ultimately dismembering him. It is said that Aguirre reveled in front of Alarcón's head on a stake, uttering incomprehensible words.

Aguirre had transitioned from being the undisputed leader to becoming a repugnant figure. The experienced and valiant soldier had metamorphosed into an agent of death. A tyrant tormented by constant fear for his life, a man who had lived in a world of betrayals and knew he would only reap more treachery. He always carried his weapons with him, probably his sword and dagger, feigned sleep but never closed both eyes; he kept one eye slightly open, watchful. He had established a guard of trust with his closest associates, but even then, he distrusted them.

Aguirre limped, his appearance was cadaverous, his countenance perpetually gloomy, and his presence, in every comment and gesture of the accompanying troop, became ominously omnipresent. Therefore, everyone feared incurring his wrath, whether through action or inaction.

In the case of Valencia, the group of marañones could not take prisoners because the city's people, already aware of the barbarity, had sought refuge on the island of Tacarigua. They had taken measures to prevent the rebels from reaching the site by not leaving any boats available. All these vicissitudes, the difficulty of the climate and terrain, constant desertions, and Aguirre's dislocated, violent, and explosive temperament had already set a date for the termination of this "cantinflesca"[48] venture.

---

[48] Famous Mexican comedian

Only a little push was needed, as Venezuelans say, for this tyrant to fall into the hands of the authorities.

Meanwhile, the forces loyal to the king were mobilizing to quell the rebellion that had sown chaos. The plan was devised at the tables of the authorities of the cities of Tocuyo[49] and Mérida[50], and the costs of the preparations would fall on the shoulders of the locals. Among those brave Spaniards willing to join the restoring force, the figure of Diego García de Paredes stood out. With his gallantry and a retinue of more than twenty men, he joined the army that was assembling under the direction of local authorities. This is where the greatness of that imperial Spain is demonstrated, where the soldier understood his duty regardless of unfavorable odds and faced the enemy in the name of his God, his honor, and his king.

Henceforth, Aguirre would not be facing defenseless and unarmed individuals, nor women and children who could easily fall prey to his violence. Now, the adversary was the local conquistadors, men seasoned in battles against the indomitable Carib Indians of the region, possessing the temperance and experience necessary to confront Lope de Aguirre. Moreover, these soldiers held an unwavering loyalty to the crown, and this

---

[49] City in the central Venezuelan region
[50] City in the Venezuelan Andes

was a period in Spain's history when it began to proudly embrace its Spanish identity.

The intricacies of the strategy were meticulously planned: where the battle would take place, how many men would be mobilized, the available cavalry contingent, and details about the weaponry. However, more than brute force, this time the governor demonstrated cunning. His first move was to strip the marañones of any resources they could exploit on their journey: no cattle were left available, cities were emptied of most of their resources, and soldiers were stationed around Barquisimeto, which loomed as the likely battleground. But most significantly, he extended an offer of pardon to Aguirre's followers, with the shrewd intention of dispersing his forces and subduing him without much resistance. Craftiness proved more potent than sheer strength, and in this case, the governor had an ample supply of it.

The plan unfolded successfully, and skirmishes gradually undermined the fervor of the rebels. In the final gasp of their insurrection attempt, when Lope de Aguirre realized that victory was unattainable, as most of his men had fled disorderly, he headed towards the place where his daughter was. With a deadly stab, he uttered his somber words:

- Say your prayers, my daughter, for I come to kill you.

- Why, my lord? – she exclaimed in bewilderment.

- I kill you, daughter, so you won't fall into disgrace, and also so they won't say after my death that you are the daughter of a traitor, – he responded coldly.

He left the room and spotted the king's forces approaching the site. However, before he had the opportunity to fight or surrender to the authorities, two of his loyal marañones executed him with precise musket shots. They likely did so to prevent the tyrant from recounting the crimes committed and accusing them of such barbarity.

His body underwent cruel dismemberment, and his parts were taken to different cities in the region as macabre reminders of the fate of traitors. The lands surrounding the place of his execution were salted, ensuring that nothing could flourish in that cursed ground. His name was condemned by religious authorities, and his soul was excommunicated, so that God's law would pursue him even after his death.

Lope de Aguirre became one of those tragic figures that seem to have emerged directly from the Greek works of classical tragedy. His destiny was already predetermined, not only by the turbulent beginning of his deranged expedition. His roots plunged their miserable foundations into a Spain that was just emerging from the Middle Ages, where poverty traced the inevitable fate of the humble.

This individual who fled Spain under the accusation of violating a peasant woman, who joined the heterogeneous group of adventurers that crossed the vast ocean, brimming with audacity, courage, and unbridled fervor but also tainted with unprecedented evil that they spread with violence in the American lands, was destined for an ominous fate. The one who was crippled in one foot in the bloody civil wars of Peru, the one sentenced to death for killing a judge in those American lands and managed to save his life by joining the king's forces to suppress a revolt, the one who finally played a role in the expedition of the marañones and with them established a country whose population was a disparate mix of thieves, murderers, enslaved blacks, and some indigenous people, could not foresee an ending other than a violent death.

However, much like the heroes of Greek tragedies who transcend oblivion, the figure of Aguirre took deep root in the hearts and memories of Venezuelans. His turbulent life and extreme actions left an indelible mark on the history of a land marked by the diversity and complexity of its narratives.

Elders and peasants of bygone eras passed down stories that sent shivers down the soul. They claimed to have heard the neighing of horses in the night and lamentations echoing from the depths of the afterlife. They asserted that these sounds announced the presence of a restless soul, that of Lope de Aguirre, known as the Tyrant, and alongside him, the wandering spirits of his marañones. They came in search of innocent souls, perpetuating their work of evil and madness in the realm of the living.

The Tyrant Aguirre continues to terrorize the people, defying the laws of God or the Devil. If anything was undeniable, it was that his spirit recognized no authority other than his own, and he was unwilling to let anyone forge a destiny other than the one he traced with his bloodstained sword.

In the vast plains of Venezuela, it is said that he manifests in the form of an ominous ball of fire, and against his influence, prayers are ineffective. The only defense that prevents his lurking is the casting of curses and the relentless reminder of his horrendous act: the murder of his own daughter. Only then, driven by remorse, does he retreat in search of a new unsuspecting victim.

I want to conclude this narrative with the account of my own father, who, in the 1950s, was immersed in the founding process of the "Acción Democrática" party in the lands of the Cojedes State. He recounted that on a warm summer night, alongside his party comrades, in the vast plains of Cojedes, they watched in astonishment as a ball of fire rapidly approached them. The initial reaction was to turn to prayer, seeking the protection of saints. However, one of those present reminded them that this appearance was characteristic of the deceased tyrant and that prayers might rather attract the attention of that demon seeking forgiveness or weakness in believers. Then, curses began to flow instinctively. "Cursed! Traitor! You killed your daughter! Agent of evil! Without God's forgiveness!" My father swore and affirmed until his last days that this event was real, and indeed, the ball of fire changed its course the moment the curses began to take effect.

The crosses of the road

Caracas – Valencia Highway, 1962

"To suffer and to weep means to live."

- Dostoyevski

The roads of my beloved land trace a map of memory, each one marked by crosses that whisper the stories of those who, in a fleeting moment, departed due to unfortunate accidents. Here, a cross at the roadside; there, a small mausoleum seemingly destined to embrace a forgotten doll. These paths of mourning are filled with memories etched on plaques, testimonies of lost love, engraved in metal and marble.

Nevertheless, the most common, simple, and austere cross stands with dignity. On its plaque, the names of those who, in their final journey, encountered an unexpected fate are respectfully inscribed. This ancient tradition, rooted in time, has endured—a tradition we carry in our hearts, a way to pay homage to those who departed in the tumult of an accident.

This introduction brings to mind the memory of a young woman, a stranger from the northern lands, who came to visit our country. Her eyes, filled with wonder, rested on the numerous crosses that lined our roads. She was not only impressed by the apparent insecurity of our roads but also by the profound meaning of this deep-rooted custom. With curiosity, in her gringo accent and broken grammar, she would inquire, "What do the roadside crosses mean?" I would reply, "They are our humble tribute to those who left us abruptly, victims of an accident." Her response, calm but tinged with sadness, was, "How sad!"

Silently, I thought to myself, "Sad is the forgetfulness that looms over the roads of the north, where the memory of loved ones dissolves in the whirlwind of life, where law and concrete dictate the course of existences." Today, from my home in Canada, I feel the strangeness of a reality that seems alien to human essence. Here, connections with ancestors fade, and death becomes a bureaucratic procedure, where, if cremation is not chosen, the body is donated to science. An accident on the road, and the country offers all the services that the technology and wealth of a nation can provide to its citizens, but memories of loved ones quickly vanish into the fabric of daily life.

- Get up! And wake the kids, we're going to be late, seriously! – shouted the wife with a distinctly "Maracucho"[51] accent.

- I'm coming, lady! Ease up! It's always the same thing. You can't do anything without shouting, without causing a scene. It's like you were born to

---

[51] accent used in the western part of Venezuela.

bother! I don't know what possessed me to marry you, with so many women out there, – retorted the husband.

That was the dynamic of the Pérez marriage. They couldn't agree on anything. The worst part was that they lived quarreling in front of the children. The woman, with a fiery temperament, had no qualms about venting her frustrations in public. Her shouts were well-known in the building, and neighbors, accustomed to these scenes, would smile and think, "There they go again, those crazies."

It wasn't clear if they hated each other, loved each other, or were simply bored with marriage because, just as they shouted at each other, they also reconciled from time to time and were occasionally seen embracing. They definitely fell outside the pattern of what we would call sanity. Some people lack the necessary maturity to form a couple and live their lives like cats and dogs. The worst part is that they transfer their dissatisfaction to the next generation because they can't express their differences in private; instead, they air them in front of their offspring. That was Gloria and Raúl.

In addition to them, there was a seven-year-old girl named Marina, a beauty with her curly black hair and an angelic face. Round eyes and a very delicate nose, with a somewhat nasal accent that wasn't annoying but added a touch of charm to her overall demeanor. Raulito, the three-year-old boy with a big head but beautiful Mediterranean features reminiscent of his maternal grandmother's Spanish family, also completed the family.

It was December, and the wife was getting ready to travel with the children to the city of Valencia, where they would stay at her in-laws' house. The plan was to spend the holidays with her husband's family, as they had spent the previous year's festivities with the wife's family. She didn't like the idea of traveling alone, but her pride prevented her from insisting that he accompany her. He, in turn, didn't make the necessary effort to join the trip and enjoy a few days of peace, away from arguments.

The husband settled for giving her a recommendation.

- Gloria, be careful. Remember, you have the kids with you, and on that highway, there are always crazy drivers.

To which the woman responded with a touch of bitterness,

- If you really cared, you'd join us instead of being stuck in that insignificant job that barely pays you.

The wife's comments wounded the man, who genuinely struggled to support the family and cover all expenses. The way she belittled him seemed absurd, as it wouldn't change the outcome of the trip.

However, from the back seat, the little girl intervened,

- Dad, we'll be waiting for you there, - and the man's face lit up. It even saddened him, as his children provided him with the peace and happiness that the marriage couldn't give. He proceeded to bless the children, a kiss for each, and a reluctant last-minute kiss for the wife.

The journey began as scheduled at 10 in the morning. Calculating that they could reach Valencia in about two hours, maintaining an average speed of 100 kilometers per hour, they were supposed to arrive by noon. Everything was going wonderfully; the AM radio broadcasted popular songs of the time, and the landscape unfolded before the curious eyes of the children. They left behind the characteristic mountainous terrain of Caracas to enter the central plains of the Aragua state. In this region of Aragua, remnants of the central mountain range could still be appreciated, opening into small valleys with exceptionally fertile lands. Since colonial times, these lands had witnessed the traditional cultivation of sugarcane and the production of rum, reaching levels of international recognition.

They approached a curve that marked the entrance to the straight road that would lead them to the city of La Victoria. Unfortunately, the car lost a tire, which shredded abruptly, unleashing chaos as the driver struggled to maintain control. That treacherous curve, in full descent, would become a tragic gorge for those who were unfamiliar with the road or fell into distraction. Events unfolded with dizzying speed. The forces inherent to this type of accident transformed the scene into chaos of erratic movements. Objects and passengers were thrown in various directions, victims of the abrupt alteration of the vehicle's orientation. They tumbled up and down, from side to side, in a frantic dance inside the car.

During that time, seat belts and restraint systems, such as the airbags we consider indispensable in rollover accidents today, were rarities. The baby was ejected through the rear window, shattering the glass in its path. The little girl, on the other hand, bounced repeatedly between the car's roof and the back seat. Gloria, in a cruel fate, shared a similar destiny. Since she wasn't wearing a seatbelt, she too was thrown out of the vehicle, through the front windshield. Then, the car trapped her against the abrupt slope of the small hill rising to the right of the road.

People traveling on the same route stopped to help the accident victims. Among them, a man, a perfect stranger with a wide-brimmed hat radiating calmness and compassion, approached the area where Gloria was trapped, still alive. Although her condition was devastating, and blood flowed from multiple wounds, Gloria found the strength to utter words amid unbearable pain:

- My babies, my babies.

The woman's suffering persisted for another agonizing thirty minutes. Repeatedly, her lips whispered the same plea as she struggled to sit up and search for her children. The distant voices of a police officer, who had already arrived at the scene, reached her ears, adding unfathomable anguish to her condition.

- Poor boy, he died on impact with the pavement, and the girl died from a broken neck hitting the car roof. This is a true tragedy, – murmured the officer.

Meanwhile, the traffic personnel proceeded with meticulousness. They carried out the lifting and secured the accident site, documenting every detail through a careful series of photographs. They captured panoramic images describing the scene in which the drama unfolded. Numeric markers, like constellations of silent witnesses, pointed out points of interest and traces. Close-up shots clearly revealed the aspects of the vehicle and the victims. Arabic numbers identified possible events, providing traffic officers with a graphical representation of the tragedy.

- Time of the accident? – the officer inquired.

- Approximately ten forty in the morning, – his colleague responded with unflinching calmness.

- How many individuals involved? – the officer asked again.

- One adult woman, around thirty-five years old, in critical condition; a girl, at least eight years old, unfortunately deceased in the vehicle; and an infant no more than four years old, ejected from the car and a fatal victim, – received another emotionless response.

However, among those present, both men and women, some tears silently slid down their faces as they witnessed the unfolding scene in the middle of the road. Gloria's final moments unfolded with the support of those trying to comfort her. The man who arrived first stayed by her side, took her hand, and offered words of solace until her last breath.

- God bless you, daughter, – said the compassionate person as Gloria's voice faded away. However, her lips continued to repeat, "My babies, my babies, my ba...

The fateful news reached Raúl while he was in his office. An officer from Civil Defense was tasked with making the call since his number was listed as the emergency contact. The person delivering the information lacked the necessary delicacy, and at first, Raúl couldn't comprehend what was happening. It took several repetitions of the tragic events for him to grasp the reality. Finally, he dropped the phone and collapsed to the floor, experiencing the deepest pain one can endure, murmuring with a mix of helplessness, anger, and sadness:

- God! Why have you done this to me?

The process of identifying the bodies proved traumatic. Raúl had to go to the morgue in the city of Maracay. No morgue is a pleasant place to visit, but Maracay's intensified the gloomy nature of these places. Ill-maintained black bars at an entrance crowded with people eagerly waiting for the opportunity to identify their loved ones. Individuals of all kinds gathered in the area, from relatives of prisoners needing to recognize the deceased in the nearby prison to those reclaiming their loved ones who had died naturally on the city streets or in the hospital, and unfortunately, also those who had lost their loved ones in traffic accidents.

Raúl was not alone, but only one person close to the identification process was allowed entry. His parents and Laura's parents had already arrived, all crying or overwhelmed by the tragedy. The wait, combined with the stifling heat typical of that city, resembled hell itself. Memories, both pleasant and unpleasant, intertwined in Raúl's mind: his children's hugs, the day they were born, the girl's communion, meeting Laura, his wife, the first time they made love, the first fights, jealousy, distrust, anger, reconciliations, but above all, the memory of that last day, the last damn fight, and the regrettable decision to let them go alone on that road. If only he had stopped her or, at least, had driven himself. He would have preferred even to die with them than to continue living.

Inside the morgue, the pathologist was already carrying out the necessary procedures. Since the deaths had occurred violently, an autopsy was necessary. The doctor made an incision from the neck to the thyroid cartilage, descending to the suprapubic region, encircling the umbilical scar. The skin, soft tissues, including muscles and aponeuroses, as well as tissues between the ribs, were carefully cut. In the abdominal cavity, the parietal peritoneum was incised, allowing access to the cavity and the search for any evidence that could shed light on this tragic accident.

The doctor recited his words with a particular solemnity:

"Feminine corpse, 34 years old, of white race, slender constitution, with a height of one meter and sixty-six centimeters. Possesses long, straight, black hair, brown eyes, and exhibits cadaveric rigidity. Multiple injuries are found on her body: multiple traumas, fractures in various lower extremities, and in the right arm. The cause of death is attributed to multiple wounds..."

The forensic doctor presented himself as a cold and meticulous individual, whose work was in no way affected by the sight of a family shattered by fate. Nor was he disturbed by the vision of children's bodies in their most gruesome form or by the figure of a woman who had experienced the final minutes of the most intense physical and spiritual pain. The story behind these corpses was irrelevant to him. His sole task was to collect data as meticulously as possible to complete a form on behalf of the public entity for which he worked.

One could say that this scene evokes the verse of José Martí[52] in his poem "The Yellow Doctor," which reads:

"The yellow doctor came

To give me his medicine,

With one sallow hand

And the other hand in his pocket."

Yes, the bodies of the deceased had become a kind of marionette, where organs that no longer served their miraculous function resembled props in these lifeless bodies. Their deformity made the skin easily contract, while the doctor, acting more like a butcher than a surgeon, proceeded to remove pieces of the organism to fulfill his role as a cold and highly technical investigator. We should not blame

---

[52] Cuban poet.

this professional for his behavior, as his work is essential, and no one else has the courage to perform this job that is extremely useful for our society. However, from the perspective of an ordinary man, this activity becomes alien to compassion and empathy.

The necessary time passed to allow the entry of family members to recognize the bodies. Raúl was not in a condition to enter alone, and his father was allowed to accompany him. The situation was extremely tense. Metal stretchers held the bodies of his family, alongside the bodies of others waiting to be recognized and claimed. Everything happened in a white room, with neon lights in a false ceiling made of plaster placed after concrete, black stains on the floors and the legs of the stretchers due to the lack of cleanliness in the place. And the smell, what a smell! It was the smell of death, of decomposition, a compilation of images and sensations that destabilized those who had never been associated with the phenomenon of death.

Raúl's father took his son by the arm, and when the official showed him the face of his deceased wife and two children, the man collapsed and cried like a child. Once again, in a moment of absolute hopelessness, he whispered:

- God! Why have you done this to me?

His father and father-in-law took care of the funeral arrangements. Raúl remained like a zombie most of the time, not because he was given medication or sedation, but because life had lost all meaning for him. He had no idea when the wake was or how the burial unfolded. He simply followed the procession without understanding much. His tears welled up from time to time, and memories of fights with his wife intertwined with the hugs of his children in his heart. Every now and then, he repeated with regret:

- God! Why have you done this to me?

People at the wake approached the chair where he sat, offering comfort and words of condolence. Raúl, alone and unwilling to engage in the scene, observed them but did not respond to their words or advice. This process only made his situation more painful, as Raúl just wanted to forget, wake up from that nightmare, or simply sleep and escape from the immense pain.

However, even in his almost hypnotic state, Raúl noticed the presence of an unknown man standing in front of the coffins of his wife and children. It was the same man with the wide-brimmed hat who had been present in the final moments of his wife. He approached Raúl with a courteous and friendly greeting:

- Good evening, – said the man with the hat.

Surprised by the presence of a stranger, Raúl responded with a – good evening.

The man took Raúl's hand and continued, – I came to pay tribute to your wife and children, as I was present during the last moments of your wife on the road.

Raúl listened attentively, his mind momentarily awakened from its numbness. Why would a stranger feel the need to honor his family? Nevertheless, he settled for responding courteously, - Thank you for being here.

Without giving him a chance to continue, the man added kindly, - I know you are going through an indescribable situation. The pain of loss is immense, and in moments like these, we face the painful reality of the fragility of life. The loss of a loved one reminds us of how fleeting our existence can be and invites us to reflect on the true value of each day. Amidst the sadness you feel, you can also find inspiration in the way your loved ones lived their lives. Forget the disagreements and the bad times and search your heart for the memories of love and the imprints they left on your existence, because that is a testament to how precious each moment is. I'm not asking you to embrace life with gratitude, I'm not asking you not to feel pain or resentment, but I urge you to simultaneously seek understanding, forgiveness, and faith that your family is still with you in a way that defies material explanation and yet is beautiful and stronger than life itself.

Without waiting for a response, the man placed a hand on Raúl's forehead and said, - God bless you. Then, he withdrew into the crowd. Raúl watched him, confused, but at the same time, he regained his impassiveness, not attaching too much importance to the encounter with the stranger.

The wake came to an end, followed by the burial, earth falling onto the coffins, and the return to dust. That beautiful woman and her exquisite children joined the cycle of life, destined to become sustenance for the beings of the earth. Raúl silently observed throughout the ceremony and did not want to wait any longer to be alone with his loved ones. He knew they were no longer there, that everything had come to an end.

Time passed, and Raúl slowly began to reclaim his life. He stopped dressing up to go out, sold his property, and moved to a smaller, more modest apartment. He distanced himself from acquaintances, disconnected from his job, his parents, and in-laws aged and also departed, and life finally marked him with the footprints of time.

It is December, and in a bed of a public hospital lies an elderly man in a delirious state with a reserved prognosis. Doctors do everything possible to limit his pain, but they know he has only a few hours, if that. The old man struggles for every breath, but he does not fear departure. He has awaited for years the release from the sentence that life imposed on him in a fateful accident on the road, a pain that marked him deeply. His last words:

- God! Why have you done this to me?

With a final sigh and a tear rolling down his cheek, his heart stops.

Silence, silence, silence.

At the crossroads of human existence, the question arises of whether we are the architects of our destiny or if, on the contrary, our paths are already outlined in the stars. Could Raúl, in a twist of events, have altered the course of events if he had stopped his wife for a fleeting moment or if he himself had taken hold of the wheel of destiny? The answer lies in the nebula of the unknown. However, it is worth questioning whether he might have the power to weave a different narrative for his life, even after the tragedy that haunted him.

We, as human beings, have become accustomed to pleading for the miraculous intervention of higher forces to alleviate our sorrows and unravel the entanglements of our lives. However, life unfolds its plot without transcendental acts that modify the conditions imposed by the future, sometimes in a ruthless manner. Life, at times, reveals itself as a beautiful symphony, but in most cases, it disguises itself in the garb of the terrible.

I can only witness that there are three new crosses, erected on the edge of the Caracas – Valencia highway, and they are the saddest memory I have of my family trips to the town of Tinaco. Those crosses, impassive witnesses to the tragedy, stand as painful monuments in life's journey, reminding us of the fragility of our existences and the unpredictability of destiny.

Silence, silence, silence. One, two, three, ...

Does evil exist?

Cabimas, Zulia state 2001

"For God so loved the world that he gave his one and only Son, that whoever believes in him shall not perish but have eternal life."

Juan 3:16

The relentless sun of Zulia yielded to neither locals nor strangers, punishing the internal courtyard of the church where the premarital course would continue with unwavering intensity. A stone bench cradled the groom, whose mind was engulfed in a whirlwind of thoughts, interwoven with conflicting emotions.

The courtyard, dotted with cherry trees that offered a hint of shade and tranquility, intersected with pavements connecting the administrative area to the church; both structures lay parallel. The betrothed, clad in dark blue jeans, a light gray shirt, and moccasins of the same shade, stood as a witness to challenging months. His relationship with his fiancée had faced adverse winds, plunging him into a state of unrest, apprehension, and insecurity. Yet here they were, bound by providential designs or perhaps by their own stubbornness that resisted accepting a no in this life.

Pausing to observe the stained glass windows in detail, the groom focused on one depicting the

Archangel Michael, clad in Roman general armor, subduing the demon with a lance. The image of the angel overcoming the demon had always struck him; the victory of good over evil, of God over Lucifer, was an axiom in his mind. Michael, God's right hand, the divine sword punishing evil, recalled the groom.

"Finally, we will complete this topic of marriage..." he reflected. "Everything has been so difficult. So many waits and delays, and this course that turns out to be somewhat tedious," he continued in his musings. "It's 1:45 pm, and the priest has not arrived yet."

Despite the intense heat, the internal courtyard of the parish offered refuge, with the scent of cherry leaves and a gentle breeze comforting the groom. Sunlight filtered softly, creating a more tranquil atmosphere in the place.

Suddenly, peace was interrupted by roars and commotion. A group of young people and a lady led a disoriented, overwhelmed girl, like a sheep being dragged. Observing from a prudent distance, the groom wondered what was happening with the group. One of them entered the offices of the administrative area and emerged with a young priest carrying a little book, possibly religious material, a Bible perhaps, along with a rosary and a small flask. A conversation unfolded; the priest interrogated the bewildered girl, but the distance prevented the words from being audible to the onlooker. Then, the priest sprayed liquid on the girl's head, and she completely lost control. The attendees struggled to contain her while the priest read from the book to the group. The witness instinctively suggested keeping a distance from that event. He did not want to ruin what had been hard-won for matters that were none of his concern.

Changing course, he headed towards the church to continue with the premarital course. Another priest was already there with the rest of the people, and his girlfriend awaited him on one of the church benches. He kept silent about what he had witnessed, even erasing it from his mind to immerse himself completely in the topic that had brought him to that place. What happened outside was another story, but it wasn't his.

At the conclusion of that day's session, the groom asked his bride to wait in the car, as he intended to discuss a matter with the priest. The young woman obeyed without attaching much significance to the matter and headed towards the vehicle. The fiancé, on the other hand, went to the administrative area in search of the priest from the earlier episode. Although he couldn't find him, he sensed the presence of one of the individuals from the event, a young, somewhat childish-looking man. From now on, we'll refer to the future spouse as "Mr. José."

- Hello, my friend, – José greeted calmly.

- Hello, – responded the young man, whom we'll call Pedro, the altar boy who assisted in the parish. A friendly young man, albeit prone to excessive talk, a detail that José would exploit quite effectively.

- Today, around 2 in the afternoon, I witnessed a situation with a girl they were carrying in their arms, and there was an encounter with a priest. Could you tell me what all this was about, what the girl's problem was? – José continued with a direct question. Pedro didn't hesitate to lay out the details and responded straightforwardly.

- Ah, you mean that hexed one. The family brought her because, they say, a demon took over her body, and not even doctors can do anything for her. I thought it was a 'quirk in the wiring,' but when the preacher came close and sprinkled her with holy water, things took a turn for the worse.

Pedro, a real folksy guy, honest in his way of speaking, didn't beat around the bush and spilled all the beans about what happened that afternoon. He also informed José that the priest couldn't do much for the girl and asked them to bring her the next day at the same time for an "ensalmamiento." "Ensalmamiento" was a local term sometimes used to describe the work done by witches or healers in terms of spiritual healing.

It became clear that the priest planned to perform an exorcism, and this time, José's curiosity overcame caution. José found the opportunity to sneak away the next day and showed up at the church an hour before the event. He met Father Rubén and explained that he was aware of the events from the previous day. His intention was to write a novel reflecting the process of exorcism, detached from cinematic exaggerations. Father Rubén, assigned to collaborate with Father Joaquín, who was in charge of José's marriage course, listened attentively.

Father Joaquín, an older priest, bore the weight of years on his shoulders. The ecclesiastical authorities foresaw the inevitable succession of his pastoral work, a witness to the transition looming with Rubén's ascent. However, over time, José discovered that the relationship between these two individuals was imbued with a certain tension—a conflict revealed in Father Joaquín's perception, who saw Rubén as too modern for his taste, deviating from the tradition he held dear. Philosophy and psychology inundated Rubén's shelves, relegating theology to a secondary role. His attitude leaned more towards youthful nonchalance than priestly discipline. But in José's mind, both men were fulfilling their roles.

It's not entirely clear why Father Rubén accepted José's presence at the exorcism. Perhaps the priest needed an impartial witness to certify the execution of the rite without compromising the person's health. José never got to know the exact reason, but the priest set the condition not to disturb the attendees or address the affected person directly. The demon, cunning in the use of words, should not find an echo in his discourse.

- The exorcist will fulfill his task, - expressed the priest. In the face of the devil's attempts to engage in dialogue, they would only present what was written in the Gospels and what was part of the ritual.

With absolute honesty, he added, - I am not a priest trained in the intricacies of the exorcism ritual; my background is more in psychology. However, the archbishop has entrusted me with the mission of helping this girl, and I will draw on my faith to do the best I can in the name of our Lord God. Certainly, father Rubén had developed several essays at the university on the influence of black magic and esotericism in Western culture and was selected, perhaps, for that unique component taken into account by the archbishop. Furthermore, he possessed the physical conditions that Father Joaquín no longer held.

But fear had seized the heart of Father Joaquín, not only in the face of supernatural forces but also in the uncertainty of not being up to the task of helping the young woman. Although he dedicated his life to serving others, his view of religious service was rooted in fieldwork, the struggle against ignorance and superstition, rather than in archaic rituals. The execution of an exorcism contradicted his beliefs, considering it an outdated rite. Although Joaquín initially volunteered to perform it, he obediently accepted the bishop's decision, just as Rubén accepted his appointment.

The discipline of the Catholic Church, grounded in obedience, that attitude that has always impressed both insiders and outsiders. An organization that endures throughout history, even more than the Roman Empire, thanks to that discipline based on obedience.

Exorcism, first session

It was a Friday laden with spiritual tension when Cristina, the afflicted, made her entrance into the sanctuary with a serene countenance. Accompanied by her mother, her brother, and the altar boy Pedro, the absence of the father was conspicuous; he had abandoned them when Cristina and her brother were just children. A sadly common reality in the underprivileged classes of Venezuela, where adversity often takes root in the humblest homes. The group was completed by the silent presence of José, a witness to that singular day.

The priest, aware of the solemnity of the moment, instructed them to enter the administrative area because, as is known, an exorcism is never performed within the temple. José, from a distant position, observed the scene, capturing the atmosphere laden with anticipation and mystery. The doors closed, marking the beginning of the ritual, and the priest, with meticulous dedication, prepared for the challenge that awaited.

Father Rubén, assuming the responsibility of the exorcism, approached Cristina with respect. Inquiring about her mood revealed a calm response, a calm that undoubtedly concealed the internal turbulence afflicting her. With gentleness, the priest invited her to sit in a chair, covering her with a purple clerical sash that encircled his neck. In his left hand, he placed a crucifix as a symbol of divine protection.

The start of the rite materialized with the sanctification of all present through holy water. Solemnity intensified as Father Rubén led the collective prayer, asking each one to recite the Lord's Prayer in unison. His hands, bearers of spiritual authority, rested on the foreheads of those present, devoutly repeating the sacred words that sought to banish the shadows lurking in the young woman's soul.

The scene, wrapped in ancestral liturgy, resonated with the strength of faith and the battle against dark forces. Although José kept his distance, the transcendence of the moment seized him, reminding him of the fragility and resilience interwoven in rituals that defy the inexplicable.

The father spoke with great seriousness:

- Father Pio,

- Father Candido

- Holy Spirit,

- Sanctify this your daughter Cristina, who has come to show her intention to distance herself from the forces of evil and return to the bosom of the Holy Catholic Church.

- Grant us the power to fight against evil.

The priest, persistent in his task, continued with the ritual; minutes passed, and the scene maintained an apparent normality. Everyone followed the prayers to the letter, including Cristina, who executed the procedure with meticulousness. However, for José, this spiritual trance was tedious and fruitless. His lack of inclination towards prayer and his scant discipline to comply with the confinement in that administrative space tested his patience. José's morbid curiosity was thwarted.

Momentarily disregarding the prayers that persisted as a background murmur, José stood up from his assigned seat. His eyes roamed the room, stopping at a desk, some religious books, and devotional paintings adorning the walls. The monotonous repetition of the rituals faded in his attention. Even, in a moment of distraction, he stumbled over a chair, briefly interrupting the ceremony, and apologized embarrassed.

Internally, José reflected on Father Rubén's words. The obsolescence of the exorcism resonated in his mind, considering the possibility of seeking the help of a psychiatrist. However, his attention shifted to Cristina when he noticed a strange tic in her gaze, an uneven blinking of her left eye.

Although he didn't pay much attention to it at first, over time, it became evident that something else was happening.

The afflicted gradually began to lose control, sinking into a singular trance. Her eyes closed, and her head swayed back and forth in a cadence reminiscent of the serene movements of a Tibetan monk reaching nirvana. The priest's prayers and those of the attendees intertwined in a ritual chorus, but occasionally, the young woman broke in with screams emanating from an internal voice, a distant and haunting tone, far from what should be the typical voice of a young person.

The chilling scene captivated José in such a way that it momentarily left him paralyzed. However, he reacted quickly, returning to his seat and joining in the prayers of those present. Cristina's brother played a crucial role, acting as physical support to prevent the young woman from hurting herself or attempting to harm those in the room. Additionally, he protected the priest from any possible violent action by his sister, as it was evident that she was trying to attack him at times. José, although he couldn't assert with certainty that he was facing a demonic presence, sensed that the girl who had entered a while ago was no longer the same as the one before his eyes.

Cristina's frenzied dance suddenly ceased, revealing a radical change in her expression. At this critical moment, the priest made a fundamental mistake, contradicting his own advice not to engage in dialogue with the afflicted. The girl, abruptly, transformed her countenance, exhibiting a mixture of sadness, fear, and uncertainty on her face. She turned her head slightly to the right, as if looking into nothingness, shrugged her shoulders, and clasped her hands over her legs. The change was so drastic that the priest, clearly affected, stopped his prayers, and the mother burst into tears.

With the solemnity that characterizes crucial moments, the priest began to question Cristina to ensure that her health allowed the continuation of the rite. The young woman's subdued tone resonated in the room, evoking compassion in José. The following are excerpts from the dialogue between the priest and the afflicted, shedding light on the disturbing development of events.

- How are you feeling? – Priest.

- Fine – Cristina.

- How long have you been here? – Priest.

- I don't know, I have no idea – Cristina.

- What brought you here? – Priest.

- That's hard to answer – Cristina.

- Can you give me any idea? – Priest.

Cristina's eyes moved from top to bottom and from right to left as if searching for the best answer, but her face showed complete unawareness of the situation.

- At the moment, I can't – Cristina.

- Whose idea was it for you to come? – Priest.

- My mother's – Cristina.

- And what happened that you came to the church today? – Priest.

Again, Cristina moved her eyes as if searching for an answer.

- My mother thought this was the best situation for me – Cristina.

- Did she tell you why? – Priest.

A few seconds of silence, doubt on her face, and then she responded.

- No one really told me why – Cristina.

- Do you have any idea why you're here? – Priest.

- Yes, I'm not like other people – Cristina.

- What do you mean? – Priest.

At this point, the priest had forgotten the steps of the ritual and had engaged in a direct dialogue with the affected person. Cristina continued with her response.

- People dislike me because..., I'm different – Cristina.

- In what way are you different? – Priest.

- I try to do something with my life that few people try to do. This influences my thoughts... and as a result, my actions – Cristina.

- What are you trying to do with your life? – Priest.

- Tell stories to people – Cristina.

- I don't understand... how can telling stories to people... have brought you here to the church? – Priest.

Her eyes moved again, but her body remained completely still.

- When I narrate stories, I express my ideas in a different way than expected... and this causes discomfort for others – Cristina.

- Do they dislike you because you express yourself differently? – Priest.

- Yes – Cristina.

During this time, Cristina proceeded to stand up, turned around, and walked towards the wall. She remained still for a few seconds, as if unaware of her surroundings, and then returned to the chair, adopting the same previous position. This peculiar behavior would repeat from time to time during the dialogue between the priest and the girl, creating an unsettling atmosphere in the room.

Another peculiar condition shown by Cristina, which could be described as uncomfortable and sad, was that while talking to the priest, her eyes moved up and down and from right to left, but her body remained motionless. This strange contrast continued to mark the interview, creating a sense of bewilderment for those witnessing the scene.

The dialogue continued in this manner until, suddenly, Cristina stopped her responses and began reciting a song. The melody, filled with sadness, filled the room, plunging those present into an atmosphere charged with emotions. Cristina's voice, at that moment, seemed to transport itself to a different place, carrying with it the heaviness of her experiences and the weight of unexpressed emotions.

Look, my dear,

With the absurd promise of the south,

My heart enchanted by you,

With the sadness of God.

I return to the placard,

To hide from everyone and from you,

To distance myself from the putrid evil

That I embrace when I feel.

Random kisses,

With the gray doctor's interview,

With alien answers of sound,

With endless sadness.

Everyone present was left speechless, and the atmosphere became tense, gloomy, and strange. The priest then resumed the interview:

- Cristina... – the priest began. How do you tell your stories in a way that upsets people?

- I can't describe in detail the way I recite my ideas, whether it's my speaking style or my message – Cristina.

- How do you know they dislike you? – priest. A long pause ensued, and the girl responded.

- My mother gets upset, and so do the doctors because of the way I look. The way I distance myself from people when I talk to them and the fact that I stand in front of walls from time to time for no reason before resuming my speech – Cristina.

- Can you give more details? – priest.

- This becomes too complicated to describe. – Cristina.

- There is nothing in this universe that cannot be sought for an answer – priest.

Cristina showed a sinister smile and replied.

- Which universe are we talking about? – Cristina.

- I don't know, you tell me which one – priest.

- It would be very difficult to explain it to you. – Cristina.

- So, you believe you shouldn't be here? – priest.

- The moment I express my opinion about not belonging here, the beings who dislike me will find a worse place for me – Cristina.

- Can you explain that point better? – priest.
Another long pause followed.

- No! – Cristina.

- But then why do you think you're in the church? – priest.

- Because I am doing things with my life that others don't attempt, and I am here because my mother thought this is the place where I can change – Cristina.

At that moment, Cristina changed her behavior again to a violent attitude, and her brother and José had to hold her while she shouted offensive words, curses, and threats against everyone.

The priest regained composure and returned to the ritual format, reciting the passage from the Bible found in Psalm 23:4:

"Even though I walk through the darkest valley,

I will fear no evil,

for you are with me;

your rod and your staff,

they comfort me."

Cristina looked at him with a contemptuous smile and then repeated,

Etiam si ambulavero in valle mortis,
non timebo malum,
quoniam tu mecum es;
virga tua et baculus tuus,
ipsa me consolata sunt

For José, the words spoken by Cristina were an unintelligible succession that resembled Latin, but he was unfamiliar with their meaning. Nevertheless, the extreme expression on the priest's face revealed the depth of the experience.

The process continued for another thirty minutes until the priest deemed it appropriate to stop, allowing Cristina to rest. It would resume the following week, following the saying, "After all, a tree isn't felled with a single blow."

After concluding the liturgy, the girl regained her composure, and the priest took his time to review and ensure her well-being. He also dedicated a few minutes to consoling and giving hope to the mother. The family left the church, and the visibly exhausted priest sat on one of the benches. He placed his face in his hands while José watched with confusion, undecided on whether to interrupt or leave without saying goodbye.

Suddenly, the priest expressed,

- I am a man of faith; I have dedicated my life to the church, and as a young man, I always had a sincere desire to help people through the word of God. Life, however, has shown me that men are capable of conceiving the worst actions we can imagine. There is that girl along with her family; they are suffering, and I'm not sure if I am the right person to help them. My faith clashes with my training as a psychologist. My will is overwhelmed by the weight of the distress of this family and the other people who come to the parish seeking help of all kinds.

He then continued,

- The husband suffering from his wife's infidelity, watching his family fall apart; the mother praying for a miracle for God to save her child with cancer; the elderly person living alone because they were abandoned by their family; the drug addict bound by the terrible sentence of drugs, and all this amidst the violence on our streets where life is worthless and is exchanged for a pair of shoes.

It was as if the priest, exhausted to the core, was unraveling a soliloquy of doubts and anxieties before José. Why him? Who was this outsider to bear the weight of his confidences? Perhaps, engulfed in fatigue, he found in José an unusual confidant, someone with whom to share his uncertainties without fear of judgment, or at least, someone indifferent to it.

Trying to inject encouragement into the priest's dismay, José exclaimed,

- I can't even imagine the hardship of your work, but at least you're trying to do something. Most people I know ignore the suffering of others. I believe you can help that girl break free from this ordeal.

The priest turned his gaze toward José, offering a desolate smile before adding,

- That's the crux of it. I'm not certain how to diagnose her situation. On one hand, she exhibits unmistakable symptoms of someone marked by some kind of trauma; that's where I break with the ritualistic norm when initiating the inquiry into her condition. The medical conclusions of her family do not persuade me. But, on the other hand, that voice, that tone oscillating between the grave and the grating. And even more so, when I recited Psalm 23:4, she repeated it in ecclesiastical Latin, the language that emerged in the early decline of the Roman Empire. I was never a scholar in my Latin classes during my time in the seminary, but I can distinguish when someone speaks to me in that language. Just so you know, ecclesiastical Latin is the one that arose from the years 300 AD when the Roman Empire was in decline. It was the Latin of the common people and does not refer to the classical Latin spoken by the Romans in the time of Caesar or Cicero. How can a young woman, lacking refined education, know a language as remote from everyday life as ecclesiastical Latin?

Faced with the last argument, José fell into silence, without answers. The priest, regaining composure, invited him to rest in his home, suggesting that if he persisted in his interest in the investigation, he was welcome to the next session.

The anthropologist

Jose couldn't banish from his mind the experience he had on Friday, and at his girlfriend's house, he shared the incident with a mutual friend named Clara. This young woman listened to him patiently, and at the end of his story, she suggested, - Why don't you talk to a friend of mine who is an anthropology professor at the University of Zulia?

- But... how do I contact him, and, what connection would this gentleman have with what I've told you? – Jose asked.

- Because I took his class as an elective, and there was a course where he detailed the beliefs of Venezuelan indigenous tribes in the supernatural world. He is a very learned man and might give you some ideas and perhaps add something to these esoteric sessions – she concluded her exposition with a somewhat sarcastic laugh.

- He has class on Mondays at 10 in the morning in the Faculty of Social Sciences – she added.

Monday arrived, and Jose went to the university to find the professor. He roamed the institution until he found the room where the professor taught his class. Jose entered as if he owned the place and sat in the farthest seats to listen to part of the class and get to know the character beforehand. No one paid him any attention, as the students were taking notes or listening attentively to the professor, and the professor was focused on his lecture.

"There is a branch of anthropology that addresses a question that may seem very simple, and that is why humans have religious beliefs, but it is not...", the professor explained and added to his discourse, "this question can be approached from many points of view, but according to some scholars, we should look at the languages that these religions use to convey their ideas. Religion is a universal phenomenon, and all of them use a type of symbolic language. In this language, it is understood that to refer to the concept of religion, one must expose the world of the supernatural, a world very different from the one we live in today, where there are gods and spirits, and the concept of good and evil is presented, as every religion has a moral aspect in its doctrine. A very well-known version is the figure of God and the devil, which are presented in both Christian and Muslim religions. Whether we believe in their existence or not is something that, as anthropologists, we cannot address, but we study their historical evolution with cultural richness." Having said this, he took a pause, looked at his watch, and added, - Well, gentlemen..., it's almost time. Please study the chapter on religious evolution in ancient Egypt, as we have an exam in the next class. Having said this, some students grumbled, and others laughed, but overall, it seemed that everyone had enjoyed the class.

He waited patiently for him to leave the room before approaching, and then made the following request:

- Professor, may I have a minute? – asked Jose with a certain shyness.

- Of course, certainly. How can I help you? – responded the learned man, with a friendly gesture.

- My name is Jose Salgado. My friend Clara mentioned your name, and I have some questions that I'm not sure if you can answer.

- Clara Astor, the one from Cabimas, right? – inquired the professor with interest.

- Exactly, - confirmed Jose, not knowing what to expect.

- Oh, well. If Clara has referred you, I definitely have a minute. But let's go to my office; there I can better hear your questions. I warn you, it's a room of only 3 square meters, quite messy, you know, the most a Venezuelan professor can have, along with meager salaries. But with all the passion for teaching, - he smiled, shrugged, and they headed towards the office.

Upon arrival, Jose could confirm the narrowness of the place: a small table in the center with two chairs, cluttered with disordered books; a shelf behind the table full of more books, and another on the left, with figures and bas-reliefs referring to various deities. They settled in, and the professor, kindly, indicated for him to start with his questions.

- I don't know where to begin, – confessed Jose.

- I would say start from the beginning, – the learned man responded in a joking tone.

- Well, last Friday, I was at the church of San Juan Bautista in Cabimas, and I witnessed an exorcism of a young girl.

The professor, with astonishment, added, – Perhaps you've come to the wrong place. My specialty is anthropology. However, I know good psychiatrists who could help that person, – he commented in a tone more playful than annoyed.

- I know this may sound absurd, and I really don't understand why Clara suggested talking to you. I understand that you are a man of science, and these things might seem like nonsense to you, but I'm trying to understand what I saw and what might come. I also want to add that the family has consulted several psychologists and psychiatrists, and none has given them a coherent answer.

The professor, with seriousness, sighed and then argued, – I wouldn't call it nonsense. Let me explain. As an anthropologist, I dedicate myself to studying the cultural expressions of peoples, and my specialty focuses on the religious aspect. Religion was an evolutionary process in humans. Before religion, our condition as a species did not differ much from that of a tiger or a horse. We ate, drank, reproduced, and at some point, when a human died, our purpose in the universe ended there. Religion emerged as a way to give meaning to our lives. Those who created it must have possessed an extraordinary capacity for abstraction to imagine the entire process after death and all those beings that controlled that universe. In fact, art and science as we know them today would not have been possible without the path previously opened by religion.

Jose listened attentively and reflected to himself, "... I don't know if this will help me understand this phenomenon, but this man truly has quality in teaching."

The professor continued his exposition,

- Today, we handle familiar concepts like freedom, will, intelligence, love, hate; all these words have a process and presuppose knowledge of the inner self of the human being. But all this has been a meticulous process of centuries, an analysis by philosophers and thinkers. It all started when some man, living in the forest, stopped to think that life must have a greater meaning. I don't see any antagonism between the work of the German philosopher Max Scheler, 'The Place of Man in the Cosmos,' and the first vision of that man from the forest. While Scheler tried to place a meaning of man in the universe using the scientific knowledge of the 20th century, that man from the forest also tried the same, but based on his intuition.

Jose, meditative, interrupted the discourse with the following question: "But then, how do you analyze the process of exorcism? Where does this ritual fit in? Is it real, or is it an imaginary process or mental illness?"

- It depends on what you understand as real or imaginary, – the professor explained.

- For example, for a physicist specializing in quantum physics, reality has many facets. They perfectly understand that a particle can exist simultaneously in different places. Our bodies are composed of millions of particles, so a first conclusion might be that you and I and everything else exist at the same time in different universes. But that is not what our brain captures or experiences. You are sitting there, and for me, it's not possible for you to exist elsewhere at this very moment. For me, that would be just the imagination of someone inclined towards science fiction, and it's not only my original point of view, but a man like Albert Einstein vehemently denied quantum physics theories. However, today it is becoming increasingly clear that quantum physicists were right, and the behavior of the universe is stranger than our brain can comprehend.

Jose observed the professor, took his time, and responded to his stance with this proposition:

- But you are using a scientific standpoint as an example, and exorcism refers to the existence of supernatural entities, God, the devil, or demons, or whatever.

- Exactly, Jose. As I told you, nowadays we know that the universe is so strange and complex that, although we cannot affirm the existence of certain phenomena, we also have no evidence to deny them. That is the function and duty of men of study, – the professor added.

- Do you believe in God? – Jose asked.

- As for whether I believe in God, I can tell you yes, but my view is based on faith and not knowledge. I want you to have a clearer perception of me or, at least, of my academic background. I also have an undergraduate degree in pure mathematics, which I pursued when I was very young, before falling in love with anthropology. I must tell you, based on my knowledge as a mathematician and according to what science predicts, the universe will have a lifespan of 8 trillion, trillion, trillion, trillion, trillion trillion, trillion, trillion, trillion years. A figure that few computers today can handle. In that universe, in its last state of life, there will be one last black hole that, inevitably, will have to expel the last portion of matter contained within it. It is at that moment that the universe we believe we know will come to an end because there will be no more entropy, and with it, the concept of time will disappear. Every law of physics we know and will know will no longer make sense. And it is at that moment when every war, every evil, every ambition, every passion, pain, sadness, anger, idea, religion, ideology, of all forms of intelligent life that can develop in that time, will cease to be important. But it is at that moment when the concept of God will be relevant in the sweet power of faith. Faith surpasses the compendium of all accumulated and yet to be accumulated knowledge, as it is based on intuition, the same intuition that scientists or engineers use to infer solutions or answers to doubts where evidence validating what is true is still lacking, but hidden from the eyes of many and few. That is where, for me, God is, and perhaps we will understand when the prophet said, 'And which of you by being anxious can add a single hour to his span?' – responded the professor.

- So, do you believe in the existence of the devil? – José continued.

- The devil! - repeated the professor with a somewhat high and sarcastic tone. He then added, - Satan, Mephistopheles, Lucifer, Fallen Angel, Beelzebub. All these names and more have been assigned to that figure. References to the devil in the Bible are actually few. Christians believe that the devil was a fallen angel who rebelled against

God and was defeated in combat by the archangel Michael. But I prefer the vision of St. Augustine.

The professor continued with a sarcastic laugh,

- First, St. Augustine gave philosophical form to Christianity by taking Plato's concepts and adapting them to Christian doctrine. He defended the existence of a single soul and the power of a single will, expressing, 'It was I myself who wanted, I who did not want; I was myself.' So, if we do something wrong, it's because we allow it. For St. Augustine, we are born sinners, hahaha, – he laughed, – I don't necessarily support everything he presented, - he added sarcastically.

The professor continued,

- For Augustine, truth is the measure of all things, and God is the truth. Truth does not accept deception, and with truth, one chooses the path of good. God is also happiness, but Augustine's happiness is based on those men who do the best with what they have. Simple and peaceful life linked to the existence of God. It is worth noting that St. Augustine was almost a man of what I call the early Middle Ages, and this is where the idea begins to take shape that laughter is more linked to sin and misbehavior, and that happiness is actually linked to a process of spiritual peace. That's why demons use sarcastic laughter to mock the ritual of exorcism.

- But... what was evil for Augustine? - the professor asked rhetorically -. Evil is the absence of God. It strips evil of all entity and excludes God, the creator of everything, from its existence. The fallen one, by distancing himself from God, voluntarily chooses the path of evil, the absence of God. So, if God is happiness and peace, the demon will be the opposite.

José listened attentively and with pleasure to this particular class from the erudite professor, but at the same time, he was left wondering if what he had seen was based on real events or was an effect of a mental illness. The professor sensed what was going through José's mind and completed with these ideas:

- In my fieldwork, I have observed things that I still cannot explain to this day. For example, a housewife who claimed to be possessed by the spirit of the Indian Guaicaipuro[53]. She did not exhibit a schizoid or paranoid illness or any visible mental affliction. However, when these events affected her, the lady would drastically change her voice tone, and her physical constitution would also be affected. Her pupils remained unchanged, and her speech was not that of the woman I had normally come to know. I have also witnessed people in extreme catatonic states, but psychiatric analyses showed no mental illness. I am not saying that these people were possessed by a demon, but they

---

[53] Historical character who fought against the Spanish conquistadors.

certainly had a condition that still has no explanation, and the ritual of exorcism acts as a kind of treatment that, in some cases, turns out to be more effective than a psychiatrist's drugs. Certainly, let's not forget that these individuals have developed in a context of beliefs that allow them to internalize these experiences as supernatural situations. Those who are distant from religious beliefs will define these events as extreme depressions, psychosis, extreme violent behavior due to mental or sociocultural issues, etc. But aren't these occurrences or ailments another expression of evil? Whether from a religious standpoint or from the perspective of an atheist, all these afflictions, regardless of what we believe, end up causing harm. We could conclude that evil exists independently of your beliefs or stances because good is directly related to the well-being of the soul and consciousness, but evil is the complete opposite. So, if you ask me if I believe in the existence of the devil, I would say yes. Because I believe that in this universe, there are two forces constantly in struggle, one being good, represented by what some call God, and the other being evil, which within our society we have named the devil.

His explanation was accurate and convincing, filled with solid concepts. Additionally, his approach to the subject was very engaging. However, it had already gotten late, and José had to return to Cabimas. The prospect of taking the bus at the terminal was not very pleasant due to the heat of Zulia, something he was not accustomed to. He proceeded to thank the professor for the time he had taken, and with a handshake, they bid farewell. Before leaving, he noticed a somber look in the professor's eyes and a final piece of advice, something like, "Be careful with what you seek because there are things that are better left where they are."

José arrived at the terminal, got on the bus and waited for it to fill up, and an image of Cristina entered his mind. At the same time, he observed the people, groups with bags and sacks in hand full of merchandise; the place seemed like a bazaar in the city of Istanbul. The faces of some Guajiro Indians crossed his view, and some approached to sell him various things through the window with the typical Guajiro accent.

- Look, chico[54], get me this watch, it's really good... it's a Rolex, – one of them said.

- Don't pay him any mind, – said another. Better off buying this cellphone from me, - retorted his competition.

The evening descended, and the temperature became more bearable. The sunlight reflected on the glass window of the seat where José was sitting. A breeze lifted the dust, acting as a natural prism that

---

[54] Buddy

tinted the late afternoon sun with a reddish hue. He felt sleepy, and the bus began its journey.

They passed by a church, and the usual beggars were at the door. Some were simple fraudsters pretending to lack an arm or a leg; others were people forgotten by God's grace who couldn't find a way out of their poverty. Inside the bus, the customary person asked for money to help a sick relative or used the excuse of not finding work. His script had been rehearsed thousands of times on thousands of bus trips of this kind, and some passengers shouted at him, "Go find a job; you're not here to be begging for money!" José smiled because he found the Maracucho accent amusing and their straightforward responses that didn't hesitate to express what they thought of the person.

The beggar got off the bus at the first stop, and the vehicle took the fast lane to head towards the Maracaibo bridge. Eight kilometers of bridge over the great lake. The sky still reflected its blues, although the evening was transitioning into night. José fell asleep, and a quick dream enveloped him. The image of the girl appeared to him. At first, she was beautiful with her long hair in a somewhat seductive pose, but then she transformed into an old woman with red eyes and a squeaky voice. He woke up startled. He assumed he had been too exposed to the topic and hoped to reach his destination. Tomorrow would be another day.

Second exorcism

On that day, José took the initiative with the intention of engaging in a conversation with the priest, a man who struck him as amiable. Unlike the archetype of the elderly clergyman who insists on preaching about God, sin, and the threats of the underworld for those who do not set foot in the church, this individual proved to be a cultivated and compassionate person. With a profound understanding of the challenges of contemporary man, he balanced his faith with the notion that the mind plays a fundamental role in the well-being of individuals.

On that occasion, the priest exuded confidence. His presence was imbued with a different aura, as if he had evolved to become the knight in shining armor ready to sacrifice himself for widows and orphans. He seemed prepared to face the dragon.

During their encounter, he inquired about José's fiancée and how his weekend had unfolded. Thanks to the details provided by the talkative chatterbox, Pedro, the priest was already aware of José's participation in a prenuptial course and the circumstantial details of his situation. Pedro, the proverbial "man of details" in the parish, had taken it upon himself to relay the information.

José shared with the priest the details of his conversation with the anthropologist and posed the question about Cristina, probing for his current opinion. The religious figure pointed out that while there were aspects of the case suggesting unresolved traumas, there were also indications of possible demonic possession. The guttural voice, the unusual strength in a slender young woman, the expression in ecclesiastical Latin, and the aversion to sacred symbols were clues that pointed towards that possibility.

"The possibility?" – José reflected to himself. "So, the priest is not entirely sure," – he continued in his contemplation.

- We shall see, – the priest interjected, interrupting the scene and rising to greet Cristina and her companions.

The young woman returned with her mother and brother. Here, I want to pause to detail the mother because emphasizing her characteristics is crucial to this narrative. The lady, around fifty years old, sported short, black hair with a balanced build, neither thin nor corpulent. Her figure denoted a well-preserved body that highlighted feminine lines. However, her face reflected the weariness of facing problems and the accompanying hopelessness.

According to Pedro's accounts, the astute altar boy who was aware of everything, Cristina's attitude worsened every day, becoming more violent and rude. She experienced episodes of incontinence and, at times, went long periods without consuming food. Additionally, her sleep pattern had faded, and she spent nights pacing in circles in her room, reciting nonsensical phrases. The neighborhood, fearful, kept its distance, and the family had been shunned as if they were a contagious disease, marking the mother's face with a clear sign of exhaustion.

The brother, about two years younger than Cristina, had a medium stature, neither too tall nor too short. His build was of medium size. The face, adorned with some freckles, displayed a pale complexion, black and straight hair. He appeared as a good, diligent, and polite young man, somewhat naive in his gestures and games. The most heartbreaking aspect was the desolate manner in which he behaved when witnessing his sister's transformation into something that was no longer Cristina, filled with genuine suffering as he sincerely felt the pain she experienced.

Finally, attention focused on Cristina, a young woman of approximately seventeen years. Her oval-shaped face radiated with a white complexion, long dark-brownish hair, and beautiful round, black eyes. It was evident she had lost considerable weight, though at some point, she must have had a well-defined body, similar to her mother's.

The priest led her to a chair, once again covering her with the purple cloak and placing the crucifix in her left hand. He sanctified the surroundings and those present with holy water, paving the way for the next prayer.

- Lord Jesus Christ, Word of God the Father, God of all creation, who gave your holy Apostles the authority to subdue demons in your name and to crush every power of the enemy; holy God, who, in performing your miracles, commanded: 'flee from the demons'; mighty God, by whose power Satan was defeated…

Cristina remained tranquil, and even those present followed the prayers as instructed by the priest, with Cristina joining in. Her expression was serene, even joyful. Everyone began to think that perhaps Cristina was healed. However, after some time, suddenly, she tensed as if a sharp pain struck her from within, then turned her face towards the priest and, with a mature woman's voice, uttered:

- You know, Father Rubén, the most difficult thing of all is that I don't even want to get out of bed anymore. I don't want to go to school or spend time with my family. Some days are better, and others are horrible. I'm tired of the voices, tired of people attacking me, tired of everything.

- Sometimes I cry when it rains, and no one notices. I draw dolls, all kinds of dolls, – she laughs with tears in her eyes.

- I like animals and drawing in the air. In the clouds, I imagine that I fly, – she smiles again, crying, and adds…

- But nothing makes me happy anymore; I don't cry, and that hurts. I don't feel alive anymore. I should go and move to the other side. There, only absolute loneliness awaits me. Nothingness, but also the end of my suffering.

- Do you have any idea what it's like to live your life first on Prozac and then on clonazepam? – she smiled faintly and melancholically.

As she expressed a series of thoughts, the priest persevered with unwavering discipline in the ritual process, paying no attention to the girl's dialogues. The attendees continued to repeat the prescribed prayers, immersed in the solemnity of the moment. The murmur of sacred words filled the room, contrasting with Cristina's bewildering interaction.

Her words flowed with an unusual cadence, as if an external force guided them. The priest, undisturbed, focused on the ritual, while the onlookers sought to understand the meaning behind Cristina's expressions. The atmosphere was charged with palpable tension, as if the boundaries between the earthly and the divine blurred in this spiritual confrontation.

The prayers continued as a constant echo, providing a sonorous counterpoint to the situation. Cristina's once serene voice now resonated with unexpected depth, as if an unknown entity used her as a vessel to convey a message beyond human comprehension.

Exorcist:

"Do you renounce Satan?"

All:

"Yes, I renounce."

Exorcist:

"Do you renounce all his works?"

All:

"Yes, I renounce."

Exorcist:

"Do you renounce all his vanities?"

All:

"Yes, I renounce."

Exorcist:

"Do you renounce sin, to live in the freedom of the children of God?"

All:

"Yes, I renounce."

Exorcist:

"Do you renounce the seductions of iniquity, so that sin may not dominate you?"

All:

"Yes, I renounce."

Exorcist:

"Do you renounce Satan, who is the author and prince of sin?"

All:

"Yes, I renounce."

Cristina watched as if it were a joke, occasionally laughing, but also crying. Suddenly, she began reciting these verses:

The world is upside down,

I don't know if you've seen.

Perhaps, it comes too late,

But I'm tired of playing keen.

The madman in the shed,

Says love is the only thread,

The one soothing his unrest,

Bringing him back to the crest.

I don't want your injection,

No more of that tranquil selection.

I prefer the flowers,

That make me smile for hours.

Tears and saliva ran uncontrollably down Cristina's face and mouth. She devoured what little remained of her nails, and her gaze, once lost in emptiness, focused on the figure of José. Her eyes fixed on him, her suffering directed at him, her anger aimed at him, her hopelessness centered on him, her fear placed on him. This sudden turn of events unsettled him, and in response, José experienced a clear loss of control. The priest noticed it immediately and called to him once, twice, three times until he finally shouted, – José, José, react. Focus on the prayer.

He had to be led out of the administrative area to the chapel to prevent the disturbance from continuing. Pedro assisted in this task, also seizing the opportunity to distance himself from the scene, as the atmosphere had become tense, obscene, and unhealthy. A strange darkness hung outside the church in a land where sunlight normally abounds, and an unexplained chill invaded the administrative area, unusual for the region.

Once outside, Cristina's screams and wails echoed in the air. The mother wept inconsolably, while the priest's voices ordered the brother to support her.

The situation lingered for another ten minutes until the priest gradually managed to bring her to a state of relative calm. The exorcism session had concluded, but the problem was not yet resolved. Cristina left accompanied by her family, visibly unbalanced. Pedro escorted them on the way, as he lived in the same neighborhood. The priest exited thoughtfully, and José felt ashamed for having abandoned the session at the moment when he was most needed.

- Father, forgive me for leaving the room and not controlling my nerves, – Jose confessed.

The priest directed a kind glance towards Jose and assured him that there was no problem. He even added, – Jose, if Peter, who denied Jesus three times and is the rock upon which this church is built, what is left for us? Then, he continued:

- You've done well.

Jose shrugged and fell into his thoughts before asking, – What do you think of what happened in there, Father?

The priest furrowed his brow and addressed the situation more as a psychologist than a priest, – I can't help but question what I just witnessed. As a psychologist, I've always sought rational explanations for human phenomena. But what we witnessed... there are elements that suggest the possibility of a malevolent entity affecting the girl. But as a psychologist, I must also explore all possibilities. Psychosis, schizophrenia, and other severe disorders can give rise to behaviors that resemble possession. The human mind is complex and sometimes manifests in astonishing ways.

- But the change in personality and the mature woman's voice that we heard, even her facial features were different, – Jose pointed out.

- The dissociative identity disorder, also known as multiple personality disorder, is a complex psychological phenomenon where a person displays two or more distinct and well-defined identities or personality states. Each of these identities may have its own set of memories, emotions, behaviors, and perceptions, – the priest explained.

- So, you're ruling out possession? – Jose asked.

- I haven't said that, Jose. We need more information before reaching a conclusion. But please, let's not rule out any possibilities. My internal struggle between faith and reason is far from over.

- Forgive me for prying, Father Ruben, and I don't want you to think I'm judging. It's just that I want to understand better. The thing is, if the bishop ordered you to perform the exorcism, and I understand that priests are bound by unwavering obedience, you seem to be conducting a session that's a mix of psychology and religion. How would this be understood within the church?... and I assure you, I'm not judging, and nothing will leave these four walls. Nor would I lend myself to criticism against your person, as I have great trust in you, but I'd like to understand.

A faint smile appeared on the priest's face, and he argued, – Just because we're obedient doesn't mean we lack common sense. God has given us intelligence to use and solve our problems and the problems of others. I, as a priest, have the unquestionable, immovable, and irrefutable mission to help people, even at the risk of being affected in my own stability as a priest of this church that I love so much. I firmly believe that one way to reach God is by fulfilling that commandment that Jesus bequeathed to us, urging us to love one another. I'm not contravening the bishop's orders, but I'm adding the knowledge I have based on my training as a psychologist.

Jose looked at him with great respect and then added, – Father, I definitely want you to be the priest who marries me to my fiancée. You're a good man, and it would be an advantage to start my married life with the blessing of someone like you.

- Don't be a flatterer, Jose. Don't make me commit the sin of vanity, – the priest said with a faint smile.

Jose responded with another knowing smile, and they continued to talk for a while about various topic. Then they said their goodbyes, planning for a third session the following Monday. The priest preferred to give Cristina time to recover and, at the same time, reflect on the situation. The connection between Jose and Father Ruben strengthened, transcending the bounds of exorcism sessions and opening the door to a genuine friendship between these two characters.

Suggestion?

José closed the book, exhausted after hours of immersion in documents from the 17th century regarding possessions documented by the church. He had traced patterns that matched Cristina's case, but the hour was already late, and the next day's work awaited him. With resignation, he closed the books, undressed, and headed to the bathroom to take a shower.

The rain was falling heavily, accompanied by occasional thunder. José hung the towel on the bathroom railing and stood for a while, observing himself in the mirror. It was then that he heard scratching noises on the wall. He diverted his gaze toward the origin of the sounds but couldn't pinpoint the exact location. "Rats?" he initially thought, although he remembered that this was one of the signs mentioned in exorcism manuals in relation to infestations.

A nervous smile appeared on his face, but he told himself, "It must be rats." Despite his nerves, he continued with the shower. Occasionally, he cast furtive glances toward the bathroom door, watching for any movement, but at the same time, he chuckled at his own fears.

He finished his shower, turned off the light, and headed to the bedroom to go to sleep. The bathroom was diagonally positioned in relation to the door of his room. Sitting on the edge of the bed and drying his feet, José reflected when, abruptly and without human intervention, the bathroom light turned on.

- Damn! – he exclaimed aloud to himself.

A noise in the wall was one thing, but a light turning on by itself was cause for deep reflection. José stood there, petrified, unsure of what to do, feeling a lump in his throat and reproaching himself for getting involved in such a strange matter as exorcism. Despite this, he tried to find a logical explanation and came up with the perfect answer: "Yes... it must be a damaged electrical contact," he thought to reassure himself.

He got up from bed, walked to the bathroom, and turned off the light. Then he returned to his room, closed the door, turning off the light once inside, and got into bed hoping to fall asleep. It took him a bit to drift into sleep, but he eventually succeeded and immersed himself in senseless nightmares.

Rraaaww! A deafening crash shattered the nighttime silence. The storm had reached its peak fury, and thunder echoed near José's house, abruptly waking him up.

- God! – he exclaimed, highly agitated.

- What was that? – he continued in his soliloquy.

He realized it was thunder because the storm continued to rumble intermittently with similar explosions. The lightning illuminated the night, and its light seeped through the window, exposing thousands of shadows in José's room. For a while, he stood watching as the large raindrops pelted the window pane. He also observed the distant lights of the city and some lone vehicle, as well as the faint neon signs in the distance. He enjoyed watching the rain, listening to the thunder, and feeling the strong wind of storms. It didn't frighten him; rather, it revealed the beauty of nature to him. He felt calmer.

- What time is it?... darn it, – he wondered as he searched for the alarm clock.

He noticed it was 3:05 a.m. He thought about having to work early the next day and how difficult it would be to go back to sleep. Nevertheless, he tried to drift off again. Minutes later, the storm had subsided, and the rain turned into a drizzle.

He was about to immerse himself in sleep when the sound of objects echoed in the kitchen. The issue was not just something falling and that's it, but rather the sound of objects being thrown or rolled continuously.

- Shit! – he exclaimed, very worried.

He couldn't find an explanation for that. A thief? It could be, but who steals in a kitchen? Again, the theory of rats? But the truth was, he had never seen mice in that apartment. José curled up in bed and asked his father's soul to protect him. He also entrusted himself to Father Pio, to whom he was devoted. He didn't want to call his girlfriend to avoid worrying her and decided to wait to see the outcome of these strange events. He felt fear but also sadness, as memories of Cristina came to mind, thinking about the terrible suffering she endured, whatever the cause.

- God, I'm scared, – he thought.

- Help me find peace, – he requested in a short and sincere prayer.

He remembered experiencing a similar event days after his father's death, and on that occasion, he also felt fear, but the immense sadness of the loss overwhelmed him. He hadn't been a good son in the last years of his father's life, despite being very attached to him as a child. He remembered that, on that occasion, tears streamed down his cheeks as he prayed for peace, and miraculously, he managed to fall asleep despite the unsettling events.

But it wasn't the only time he had experienced similar events. He recalled the horrible nightmares of his childhood that would make him get up at midnight in tears, searching for his father and mother. He also brought to mind his time in the army and that occasion when, at the boundary between the dream world and awakening, he found himself surrounded by elders who caressed his head and mentioned the word "poor thing." Yes, a poor thing, it was a difficult time for him. He was in the wrong place, in a life that wasn't his. The strange thing about that event is that he had the idea that those people were some of his ancestors he never had the chance to meet in life. The peculiar thing is that he didn't feel fear; rather, he experienced a kind of kindness in those actions.

This time, the result was similar after seeking peace and tranquility. He decided not to investigate the cause of this event and, almost miraculously, managed to fall asleep.

Cristina

In the scarce moments of tranquility, Cristina settled into the living room sofa, sharing the stillness with her mother and immersing herself in the familiar atmosphere. On that particular day, she sought distraction within the pages of a novel while alone in the room; meanwhile, her mother busied herself with dinner preparations. In an unusually serene state, she relished the sense of well-being after a satisfying lunch and a morning stroll under the warm Zulian sun.

Despite the curious glances from neighbors, who regarded her as an uncommon being, Cristina remained unaffected; she felt complete within herself. However, what transpired during her good day faded away as she closed the book in her home's living room, allowing herself to plunge into childhood memories. In that very setting, at the age of seven, she returned from school to find her mother on the same sofa. Back then, her mother appeared notably younger, remembered as a charming figure that embraced her tenderly and lifted her into her arms, providing that incomparable feeling of protection and care.

Nevertheless, the present held an abrupt twist. A piercing pain in her abdomen interrupted her recollections, bending her over herself as she emitted a dry moan. Upon raising her gaze, she was met with a horrifying vision, a presence not physically there but manifesting in shadows, discordant noises, and contorted faces.

- Mom! Mom! Mom! – she cried.

The mother, abandoning her tasks in the kitchen, quickly responded to her daughter's call. The terror enveloping Cristina reached such intensity that it prompted involuntary reactions; the girl was overwhelmed, urinating and defecating in the middle of the living room. Amidst heartbreaking sobs, her eyes reflected a fear so profound that it resonated in her mother's soul, who, powerless in the situation, also wept.

The silence in the room was shattered only by the harrowing sounds of shared distress. The mother knelt beside Cristina, attempting to embrace her with the same tenderness as in those childhood days, seeking to soothe the torment unraveling within her daughter. However, the invisible presence continued its macabre dance, casting shadows that darkened the young girl's countenance.

Amidst desperation, the mother, with eyes clouded by tears, clung to the hope of finding some relief for Cristina. Helplessness and bewilderment intertwined in the room, like a tangle of uncontrollable emotions. Reality and nightmare merged, blurring the boundaries between the tangible and the imaginary, as mother and daughter faced together a horror that defied all logic.

- Oh my God, daughter! What's happening, child? – her mother cried.

Cristina, on the brink of revealing her darkest side, seemed possessed by a rage and violence that threatened to unleash upon any target. This time, the mother was alone with her, fully aware that her daughter's strength would escape any attempt at containment. Despite this knowledge, the mother, in an act of incredibly noble courage, suppressed her own fear and clung to her daughter with determination.

In a tight embrace, the mother surrounded Cristina's body, who still wept amid agitated sobs. Despite the internal storm enveloping the young girl, the mother did not yield to fear. Instead, she whispered words of affection into Cristina's ear, as a desperate attempt to break the chains of fury that threatened to consume her.

Loving words intertwined with chaos in the room, creating a striking contrast between Cristina's emotional tempest and the apparent calm of the mother. Though aware of the unpredictability of the situation, the mother persisted in her attempt to be the anchor that brought her daughter back to reality. The embrace became a link between love and desperation, as both struggled against the shadows clouding Cristina's mind.

- There, there, my girl, mama is here, my baby. May the Virgin protect you, my darling, mama is here, my baby.

Cristina roared, insulted, convulsed.

- You bitch! You're a bitch, I'm going to kill you, – Cristina said.

But the mother insisted patiently and with immense love in her attempt to calm her. Peace gradually took its turn, and the girl's roars subsided. Profanities were replaced by crying and then small whimpers. The mother picked her up and cleaned her to take her to bed. A while later, the brother arrived to witness the scene where his mother cleaned up the mess of feces and urine. The boy, with tears in his eyes and without saying anything, helped his mother.

That night, mother and daughter shared a bed. Cristina defecated and urinated in her clothes again, but she slept. The mother embraced her. Cristina's breathing was difficult; the mother took her pulse and was on the verge of breaking down. However, they were very poor and had no resources to go anywhere, besides being outcasts in the rest of the neighborhood, so they would not get help from anyone. The lady thought that night her girl would die, so she embraced her as when she was a child.

The smell and the dirt didn't matter to her; Cristina was still her baby. Love above all else. The girl regained composure; her breathing stabilized. It can be said that God was there.

Third exorcism

It was already Monday, marking the beginning of a new exorcism session for Cristina. This time, José arrived almost simultaneously with the young woman and her family. Together, they headed to the administrative area, where Father Rubén welcomed them cordially, ready as always to perform the ritual. He placed Cristina in the usual chair and covered her with the ecclesiastical stole.

The priest initiated the rite once again, with each prayer followed by the responses of those present. In the first few minutes, Cristina showed no signs of reaction, repeating the pattern of the last two sessions. However, she eventually began to experience a personality split, accompanied by a trance state in which her body, neck, and head moved synchronously from back to front.

Finally, she halted her movements and became motionless, only to lower her face and emit a sharp scream of pain. She hunched over and, in an extreme shift, expressed with a calmer voice...

- Mom, I'm scared. The voices.

- What's happening, Cristina? – the anxious mother asked.

- The voices, it might happen, it might happen, – she repeated the same phrase.

- What might happen, my daughter? – the mother inquired.

- The voices, mom, their insistence. Something bad might happen.

While this unfolded, the father adhered to the protocol and refrained from intervening in the dialogue. Suddenly, he switched to a more violent and erratic personality where the dialogues made no sense.

- Where's the bug... huh? Where's the idiot? Not studying, I know she's not studying.

Following this, Cristina lowered the tone of her voice to a more withdrawn, depressive, even beautiful style, expressing with melancholy:

- In the shadow of my being, I find a lament that entwines my soul like ivy. The shadows around me bear witness to a profound pain, an ethereal echo of suffering that consumes me. Why does this torment persist in my existence, like a dark curtain covering the light within me? I could end my life, – she added, releasing a sweet and small smile after these last words.

Her voice, though calm, resonated with a sadness that hinted at the internal struggle Cristina was experiencing. The room filled with the weight of her words as Father Rubén and the others watched attentively, not quite understanding what was happening.

The expression on the father's face was one of despair as he realized he couldn't alleviate the girl's suffering. At a certain moment, he halted the ritual and, with seriousness, responded to Cristina's last insinuation:

- Why would you try to do that? – the priest asked.

- Because I don't want to face anything, – Cristina replied with a sweet, almost inaudible voice, her face suddenly illuminated by a fleeting beauty.

- You've tried it before, – the priest stated.

- Yes," Cristina nodded, almost like a little girl, tilting her head up and down.

- How many times have you tried? – the priest inquired.

Cristina lowered her face to the left, and with a blue sadness, she looked back at the priest. However, with her face slightly tilted to the right, she uttered the words, "Several times now," and the phrase echoed in the room like a sweet whisper.

- Why do you try to end your life? – the priest asked.

Cristina moved her eyes from left to right, as if searching for the right answer. She lowered her face a bit and then released a response slightly more intense, not indicating anger, just with a more determined nuance - "I'm desperate, I can't face things... – She shrugged and added, with a voice laden with resignation: – Things that have come up, so I think the easy way out is to end it all.

The silence in the room became even more palpable after these confessions. Father Rubén's face displayed a mix of concern and compassion. The room seemed to hold a universe of emotions and secrets as everyone waited to see what Cristina's next response would reveal.

- Have you tried talking about this with your mother? – the priest asked.

- When I was little and before my father left us, I tried to get my father's attention. I threw tantrums, broke things, but nothing worked. All I achieved was letting other people, including my mother, see how hurt I was, and I really didn't want them to notice, so I tried to do the opposite, act like nothing mattered. That worked because people believed that nothing mattered to me.

After this last response, Cristina shifted to her most violent state and erupted into roars and extreme offensive language. José and the altar boy had to restrain her, but the priest approached the girl, took her face in his hands, and almost pleadingly asked,

- Tell me, daughter, what's happening, tell me what's going on, how can we help you?

After saying this, the priest pulled her close to his chest with an incredibly tender embrace, repeating the same question with calm determination.

Cristina resisted the embrace ferociously. She roared, screamed, fought, uttered insults, but the priest persisted in his actions. He held onto her with determination, like a beacon of compassion in the midst of the storm of emotions enveloping the young woman.

The scene unfolded like a conflict between invisible forces, as the priest persisted in his effort to free Cristina from the shadows that imprisoned her. The room was filled with intense energy, waiting for some glimmer of hope to break through the dense darkness surrounding the young woman.

- Tell me, Cristina, what happened to you? – the priest shouted.

- Go to hell, stupid priest, – the girl responded.

- Tell me, girl, what happened to you, I know you're in there.

- Noooooo!, go to hell, abuser, don't touch me. I told you not to touch me, don't do it.

Suddenly, the girl lost her strength, and the priest allowed her to relax, observing as she tended to lie down on the floor. Amidst a crying spell that reached levels of melancholy, she confessed:

- I wasn't to blame, Mom, I wasn't to blame. I fought as much as I could. I told him no, but he insisted. He hit me, threatened me. I wasn't to blame. My dad didn't come; he didn't come.

The girl cried, but this time it was the Cristina everyone knew. There was no strange voice, no psychotic response; this time, it was an honest and direct response, a very focused, well-thought-out plea for help. The priest took her in his arms and assured her that everything was okay, that he and her family were there to help. He guaranteed her that no one would harm her and that everything would be fine because no one had the right to judge her.

It was evident that Cristina had been a victim of abuse, an offense, an outrage. She never had a father to protect her and assert her rights. With a very young brother and in a neighborhood that more resembled a jungle, boys took advantage of any Cristina that fell into their hands. The girl who had always been the model child faced the world's cruelty and, whether to spare her mother distress or suffering, had sunk into a world of psychosis and demons that well concealed this stain.

José sat on a nearby chair, tears in his eyes, feeling a vicarious shame. He even saw himself reflected in that cruelty where men view women as prey to possess. The wickedness of humanity had stained that girl, and her wounds had estranged her from the world of sanity. The good intentions and sound judgment of a priest, along with the infinite kindness of Cristina's brother and mother, had kept her tethered to this world and brought her back to the realm of consciousness.

About twenty minutes passed, Cristina sitting in a chair, embracing her brother. The priest's suggestions regarding the most suitable treatments for the girl continued. The whirlwind of roars and discordant voices had completely ceased; Cristina experienced a sense of liberation both within herself and in her appearance.

As the days slipped away, José chose to go to the church accompanied by his fiancée. Upon arrival, he saw Cristina resting on the courtyard threshold, bathed in the radiant sunlight of the Zulian afternoons, which bestowed an intensely colorful palette to her surroundings. The leaves of the trees seemed greener, the wild fruits and mountain flowers redder, the outlines of the temple and stained glass whiter... and what beautiful stained glass windows! José's attention was once again captured by the depiction of Michael triumphing over the devil, echoing the idea that goodness can prevail from time to time.

On the other hand, Cristina's presence took on a new dimension. Adorned in a white dress accentuated by black circles, she exuded flirtation. A touch of makeup on her face gave a rosy hue to her cheeks. Her skin, now regaining the sun's glow, no longer trembled in her hands. Although some signs of time marked her face, nothing that the passage of time couldn't purify. A sweet smile adorned her countenance, intensifying when Father Rubén approached to greet her. José, on the other hand, remained in the background, keeping a distance to not disturb the delicacy of the scene.

Once Cristina left the place in the company of her family, José approached Father Rubén to greet him. They talked about various things, including Cristina's encouraging state, according to Father Rubén. There was a moment of silence, and José asked the priest:

- Father, what do you think happened to Cristina? Was it a possession?

- To be honest, I have no idea, and I don't care. The important thing is that Cristina is well... don't you think?

José nodded with a faint smile, but after a while, he asked:

- Do you believe in the existence of the devil?

- Of course, Jose. In every betrayal, abuse, lust, violence, selfishness, he is present.

- But then, do you think this was just an event of psychosis related to a mental illness? – José continued.

The priest looked at him and continued with a kind gaze:

- What were you expecting to see, José? A devil with horns, shooting fire from his eyes, and with a long tail? Do you think such an ancient and perfect entity would be so foolish as to present itself so obviously?

Jose stared into space for a while and then shifted his gaze back to the priest, asking with some doubt:

- But do you believe in God?

- In God... of course, I believe in God, José. Because God is in every new dawn, in the innocence and imagination of children, in Cristina's smile with the hope to keep fighting, in a mother's love for her daughter, in the constancy of friendship, and in so many other good things that do exist in the world. There is God because God is even more perfect than the devil, but unlike the demon, he doesn't hide; rather, he shows himself to us in all these forms. But in our imperfection, we are incapable of noticing it.

José smiled with satisfaction, and accepting the priest's invitation, they headed to the church to give thanks for this new day.

The End

www.ingramcontent.com/pod-product-compliance
Lightning Source LLC
Chambersburg PA
CBHW051510030726
47592CB00006B/2192